I am Juliet

JACKIE FRENCH

# I am Juliet

Angus&Robertson
An imprint of HarperCollins*Publishers*

**Angus&Robertson**
An imprint of HarperCollins*Publishers*, Australia

First published in Australia in 2014
by HarperCollins*Publishers* Australia Pty Limited
ABN 36 009 913 517
harpercollins.com.au

**HarperCollins*Publishers***
Level 13, 201 Elizabeth Street, Sydney NSW 2000, Australia
Unit D1, 63 Apollo Drive, Rosedale, Auckland 0632, New Zealand
A 53, Sector 57, Noida, UP, India
1 London Bridge Street, London SE1 9GF, United Kingdom
2 Bloor Street East, 20th floor, Toronto, Ontario M4W 1A8, Canada
195 Broadway, New York NY 10007, USA

National Library of Australia Cataloguing-in-Publication data:

French, Jackie, author.
  I am Juliet / Jackie French.
  ISBN: 978 0 7322 9798 5 (paperback)
  ISBN: 978 1 4607 0086 0 (ebook)
  For children.
  Juliet (Fictitious character)—Juvenile fiction.
  Shakespearean actors and actresses—Juvenile fiction.
A823.3

Cover design by Christa Moffitt, Christabella Designs
Cover image by Lucia Rubio
Author photograph by Kelly Sturgiss
Typeset in 11/17pt Sabon Ltd Std by Kirby Jones
Printed and bound in Australia by McPhersons Printing Group
The papers used by HarperCollins in the manufacture of this book are a natural,
recyclable product made from wood grown in sustainable plantation forests.
The fibre source and manufacturing processes meet recognised international
environmental standards, and carry certification.

*To Angela, with love and gratitude,
and to the angels of Monkey Baa Theatre Company
who continue Rob's magic*

# Chapter 1

ROB

**Beare Tavern, 1592**

The tavern room smelled of chamber-pots. Rob Goughe, youngest apprentice actor of Lord Hunsdon's men, scratched a louse bite under his cap. 'Out, damn spot,' he muttered. A night as lousy as his hair! Black specks in the bread he suspected were mouse droppings, not currants. A pimple as big as a baked onion on his chin. And this new script of Master Shakespeare's ...

Rob stared at the paper covering the table. Words! Page after page, scribbled so fast Master Shakespeare hadn't bothered to blot the ink. Southwark crowds didn't want speeches. They wanted dancing bears. Sword fights! They'd throw rotten apples if the company tried to give them a play like this. Or oyster shells, which were worse.

Shakespeare should have stuck to making gloves. Gloves lasted for years. Plays vanished when the audience left the ale-house courtyard. The company moved on to other tales, the old scripts eaten by the mice.

Aha! His fingers found the louse. Rob squashed it on the table. He picked up the manuscript again. *The Tragical History of Romeo and Juliet*. He began to read it properly, trying to see the action in between the words. If there were enough sword fights, they might get out of this without rotten egg on their faces and with a few pennies in the box.

Some jokes and a fight to begin with. Good. The more blood the better. A dozen jars of strawberry jam mixed with wine dregs and there'd be 'blood' smeared across the stage. Maybe this play would work despite the speeches.

He lifted the next page. No bears yet. Pity. Old Bruin dancing on his rope was always good for a laugh.

And then he saw the first line of his part, Juliet. A girl's role. Again.

Rob sighed. He always had the girl's role. Always would, till his voice broke. 'Show us your merkin, darling,' the drunks cried as soon as he minced onto the stage, trying not to trip in his long dress. 'Let's see your legs, darling.'

At least there were never many lines to learn. Mostly he just had to stand there and let the older actors speak. What could a girl say in the world of men? Except Queen Bess, of course. But queens were different.

Rob nodded as the girl let her mother and the nurse do the talking. '*Madam, I am here. What is your will?*' Yes, he could say that in a girl's high voice, eyes down.

He dipped a crust of bread in his ale. Another fight scene. Excellent. A banquet. That meant fine costumes, second-hand from the Earl's household. The commons liked gaping at silks and velvets, even if the moths had eaten the fur trimmings. Maybe they could add a dancing bear at the banquet.

Now it was time for Juliet to speak again.

The bread dropped from his fingers. Rob stared at the words in front of him.

'*For saints have hands that pilgrims' hands do touch ...*'

Words of passion and determination. What was Master Shakespeare doing, giving a thirteen-year-old girl lines like this?

Rob flicked over the pages. Marry, the girl was the hinge on which the whole play turned.

'*Then have my lips the sin that they have took.*'

He'd have to kiss Master Nicholas, in front of everyone. He'd have to stare at him with love and longing. He'd have to play a girl who defied her parents. Who proposed marriage to a boy she had just met! Who plotted to pretend to be dead so she could run away with him, all for love ...

He couldn't do it. He didn't have the experience to play a role as big as this. What did he know of girls in love, except that they'd never been in love with him? He'd never been close to a girl, except that time up in the hayloft and not much had happened then. His sisters had died of the plague long before they'd reached thirteen. Ma had died too, and Pa had married again, which was why he'd sold his son to be an apprentice to Master Shakespeare, to get a piece of silver in his pocket and one less mouth to feed.

He'd need to be a journeyman actor in his twenties with a share of company profits before any girl would notice him and he could be wed.

A man bellowed for a lackey to remove his boots in the room next door. Rob could hear drunks singing in the tavern below, the cries of oyster sellers, the lad offering to whip Bruin to dance for threepence. This was his world. Not back in old Verona.

Rob looked again at the parchment. So many words!

And yet, what words.

'*My bounty is as boundless as the sea,*

*My love as deep; the more I give to thee,*

*The more I have, for both are infinite ...*'

A breeze blew up from the river, through the rotting shutters of his window. It was almost as if he smelled roses and the taste of love amid the stench of chamber-pots, the river mud and mouldy cabbage stalks.

Suddenly he could see her. Short, like him; quiet, with eyes downcast. But inside she was a girl of fire and steel.

The night stretched into silence. The candle guttered. Even the yells of the drunks receded as he read on.

# Chapter 2

## JULIET

The bloody head thudded over my garden wall at midnight. The noise woke me just as the church clock chimed twelve. Someone laughed in the street outside.

I pushed back the bed curtains. The marble floor under the rush matting was cold as I stepped out onto the balcony to investigate the noise. Nurse snored in her truckle bed behind me, loud as the carter's horse grunting up a hill.

Moonlight lit the garden. I saw the shadowed rose bushes, the gravel paths, the high stone walls. I saw the white face of what had once been a man. Even in the moonlight I could see the blood.

I had never seen a severed head before. I had never seen a dead body. Dead bodies belonged to the world of men, beyond my garden wall.

I could smell the roses in the garden, the cold stone scent of night. Far off I heard the watchman's cry, 'All's well.' But watchmen only patrolled those streets where all *was* well. They had not helped the man whose head lay in my small garden.

A nice girl would scream and call for help. I am Juliet Catherine Therese Capulet. I am a nice girl, or at least I can pretend to be. But sometimes my thoughts and dreams are not nice at all. I peered across the shadows. Were the murderers lurking beyond the garden wall?

I knew the dead man's face, despite the blood, and those wide unseeing eyes. I had seen him in the crowd at the harvest feast on our estates, when my father made a present to each man in our service. A florin to a stable lad; ropes of pearls to the sea captains whose trading ships made our house rich. This man had been one of many hired to wear our livery of green and gold and to accompany members of our family through the streets, carrying his shield with a short sword by his side to make a good show and face our enemies.

Now our enemies had killed him. Montague rats had taken this man's life.

The laughter came again, farther away now. The Montagues had dumped the head here to make the only daughter of the Capulets scream, have nightmares.

I did not scream. I did not even pull the bell rope to call for help. If I pulled the rope now, the whole house would be gossiping that young Juliet had seen a severed head, was swooning and sobbing in her room. By mid-morning it would be about the marketplace. The Montagues would win.

I had no need of help; nor did that poor man there, though his wife, his mother, his children perhaps, would need it. We would give him revenge too. I hoped there would be Montague blood on the cobblestones tomorrow.

Girls are little use, except to marry and breed sons. My father had no son, since my brother died of the white flux when he was four. My mother's nephew was my father's heir now. I could not help my father fight his enemies. But I could help him hate them.

Better to pretend I had not seen that poor drained face. The house watchman would find him on his rounds. He would carry the head to rest decently with its body, wash away the necklace of blood. In the morning there would be nothing in my garden, except the echo of the laughter of the Montagues.

I slipped back into my room. I'd tell no one. Who was there to tell? Nurse, who would gossip? The maids, who would shriek? I saw my mother and my father rarely, only when they called for me. I had no friend, no sister.

So I went back to bed. I slept. I dreamed, but not of blood.

I dreamed of love.

Most dreams are shapeless. The pieces cannot be put together. These dreams were moments ripped from time.

His hair was dark. I never saw his face. I never even saw him clearly. Once, when I was five or six, I dreamed I threw my ball at him, hoping that he'd catch it. But the ball never reached him. It was as though he was on one side of a mirror and I was on the other.

I was ten when I knew that I loved him.

He would be tall, like my mother. Handsome, like my father. But even though I saw him sitting in the great square before the Cathedral, laughing with his friends, he was in shadow, so I could never quite make him out. Tonight, in my dream, I stood on my balcony. There was no bloody head among the roses. Instead, he was in my garden, shadows and laughter. I couldn't touch him. But I could speak.

'Goodnight!' I whispered.

I reached out ...

# Chapter 3

Nurse dropped the poker and I woke up. My dream vanished, to the place where dreams sleep when we are awake. Love vanished too. A Capulet marries for duty, not for love, except in dreams.

I glimpsed Nurse through the bed curtains, muttering to herself as she picked the poker up again and tried to get flames from the coals in the fireplace. 'Poker, poke it, poke your nose, where are those girls?'

She blew the whistle for the servants. I heard the bustle of the maids, my Joans. Joan herself was as fat as Nurse but ten years younger. Janette was a cousin of our steward, and Joanette, the youngest, was only ten years old, her face dusted with scars from the smallpox, but not too deep. My mother would only have fair maids serving in our house; no hunchbacks or birthmarks.

Nurse lifted her skirts to warm her bare backside at the sulky flames. She glared at Joan. 'You think this is a fire? It's got no more heat than a pimple on a butcher's bum. Fetch wood, and warm water for your mistress.'

Nurse pulled back my bed curtains, leaving a thumbprint of soot for Joanette to remove later. 'Are you awake, my little plum? And a good day it is too, if those lazy girls bring wood …'

I let her words flow over me. Nurse burbled every moment of the day till she lay down on the truckle bed at night. And then she was only silent till she snored.

I stretched on my feather mattress and waited till there was a gap in her words. 'I'm awake.'

'Well, up you come, my dumpling.'

I stood on the rush matting and let Nurse take off my shift. Joanette arranged the screens to stop the draught, and Joan brought a bowl of warm, rose-scented water. They washed my face, my hands, my armpits and my legs. A cloth warm from the fire to dry me; a dusting of orris root powder under my arms and across my body to make my scent sweet and soak up any sweat.

I held my arms up so they could dress me. A smock in fine white linen, a yellow silk underdress, then red sleeves pinned onto it. I lifted one leg for a cotton stocking, and then the other, then lifted them again for my silk slippers: red embroidered with green thread. Did the Joans know about the bloody head in the garden? Were the servants whispering about it in the hall? Or had the watchman disposed of the body before anyone could gossip?

They gave no sign that they knew there had been trouble last night. Joan and Janette lifted up my overgown, a loose one for a day at home, and lowered it over my head, then pinned it to the underdress.

Janette unplaited my hair, then brushed it a hundred times to keep it clean and glossy. Nurse herself plaited the thin side plaits, looped them up and then bound all my hair except the side plaits in a clean white linen coif.

I stood there as I had stood for thirteen years and let them tend me, as a nice girl should. Sometimes I thought I existed only from what they made. Was Juliet Capulet just her maids' and nurse's dressing, her dancing master's skill, the years of practice of pretty phrases such as a lady used?

No, I thought. At the centre there is me, just like an apple has a core.

At last it was done. My stomach gurgled. I grinned, and felt the gloom depart. My stomach at least was mine.

Nurse laughed. 'Listen to her! Oh, she's always had a grumbling tummy, ever since she was a babe.'

The Joans carried in the food and set it on the table: a jug of fresh ale, which Nurse warmed by thrusting the red-hot poker into it, a tray of manchet bread still steaming from the oven, glass bowls of strawberry jelly, butter, honey, a platter of cold guinea fowl, a cheese, a chicken.

I dipped bread into the ale. It was all I wanted.

Nurse clucked her tongue. 'That's not enough to keep a mouse alive! A girl needs meat on her bones. Men like plump hips, my lambkin.'

If I grew any plumper, Nurse would have to let out my petticoats again. But I took the leg of chicken she handed me, and then some of the jelly with a sucket spoon. Nurse watched approvingly.

I felt someone else watching me too. I turned to see my cousin, Tybalt, in the doorway. He was tall like my mother, his blond hair shining on his shoulders. He was ten years older than I and had been part of our household as long as I could remember. A few years hence, Tybalt and I would be married. It was something we all knew, but no one talked about, like my father's mistress or the white lead my mother put on her face to make her skin so smooth.

Tybalt was handsome, with the confidence of a man to whom fate had given everything he wanted. What it didn't give him, he would take. He had given me a puppy, Rosemary, when I was five. When Rosemary choked on a chicken bone, he gave me a lovebird to make me smile. But the lovebird made Nurse sneeze, so now it chattered in a cage out in the garden. Once we were married, and all that was mine became his, Tybalt would probably no longer give me gifts. A husband may treat his wife how he likes. But as long as Tybalt got what he wanted, he would stay sunny. And I would do my duty, to my husband and our house.

He smiled at me, his eyes watchful, excited. So, I thought, Tybalt's rapier tasted Montague blood last night.

His wolfhound sat at his feet. Threads of drool dripped onto the marble floor as he smelled my breakfast chicken.

Tybalt took off his hat — a new red one, with two feathers. He made me a neat bow, then came and gave me a cousinly kiss on the lips. 'You taste of strawberries. Down, Brutus,' he added, as the dog began to sniff my skirts.

I nodded to Janette to fill a cup of ale for him. 'You taste of last night's wine. Are you out late or up early, cousin?'

'Up with the lark's song.' He took a chicken leg and sprawled on the cushions on the other side of the table, eyeing me and showing off his legs in green silk stockings. 'You have an appetite for breakfast?'

His question was too casual. Brutus reached out a long red tongue and took some of the meat from his master's fingers. Tybalt fondled his ears absently.

'I always have an appetite,' I said.

'Indeed she does,' said Nurse. 'Oh, such a hungry one she was, even as a babe. I remember when she tore my front buttons to have her drink.'

I washed my fingers in the dish of rosewater and held them out to Nurse to dry. Little Joanette gave me a quick curtsey.

'Yes, Joanette?'

'My lady, have you finished?'

'What? Oh, yes.'

I left the table so Nurse and the Joans could breakfast on my leftovers, and sat on the cushion by the window. Joanette piled her bread with meat. She had come to us starving, her whole family dead of the smallpox. She could never eat enough now.

I glanced at Tybalt, then picked up my tapestry for something to occupy my hands. 'Well, cousin? Did you come just to share my breakfast?'

Tybalt let his wolfhound lick his fingers, then wiped them on the tablecloth. His hand shook slightly. From anger? Tybalt's furies could last for days.

'I would speak privily with you, cousin.'

I nodded, and stepped out onto the balcony, where the Joans couldn't hear us. Nurse, still chewing bread and chicken, came too, as Tybalt knew she would. I had never been away from Nurse since I was first given to her to suckle. Tybalt knew Nurse would not speak of what he told me. Or rather, she would always speak, but her chatter could also cover up what she chose not to tell. I trusted Nurse as I trusted my own life.

I tried not to glance over at the garden wall where the severed head had lain. 'What is so important?'

Once again his voice was too casual. 'You weren't disturbed last night?'

Disturbed? I had cried four tears, perhaps, for the dead man's family before falling back to sleep. How could I have wept more for people I did not know?

Should I tell him that I had seen the dead man's head?

No. Tybalt would rather be shredded by Montague rapiers than let a Montague even walk across my shadow. But I didn't trust his temper, or his tongue. There was anger simmering under Tybalt's smile. I didn't want to make it worse.

'I slept well. And you?'

He shrugged. 'It is no matter.'

I gazed out at the rose garden, at the city's breakfast smoke sifting up beyond our garden walls. 'Are you going hunting today?'

'What should I hunt?'

I had an image of a pile of bloody heads, all belonging to Montagues.

I met his eyes. 'The Montagues. Their heads, their hearts, their hands.'

For a few heartbeats I felt part of our family, part of the feud that ruled our lives. Shared hatred tasted sweeter than apples.

Tybalt's eyes brightened. 'I love you, dear, sweet cousin. The Montagues will indeed be hunted today.' He lifted my hand and kissed it, just as if I had been a woman, not a girl. 'I will bring you the caps of two Montagues, though I will spare you the heads that bore them.'

Then he was gone. His dog followed, with a last longing look at the chicken bones.

# Chapter 4

Tybalt hunted. I had to dance.

No father would employ a young dancing master for his daughter, but Master Dance looked as if he were made of sawdust, so old a breeze would blow him back to dust. His legs were like a sparrow's in his cotton stockings.

We practised. Little Tom, the apprentice minstrel, played his mandolin to keep the time. The Joans and Nurse made up the numbers for a set, and Joanette giggled every time Master Dance's corset creaked.

At last he left, still creaking, with a honey cake from Nurse to sweeten him. We sat on our cushions and worked our tapestries; or rather the Joans twiddled their needles and threads, and Nurse burped gently after her morning ale, while I stared at the garden and thought about Tybalt fighting Montagues, about the dead man's widow and his children. Were they weeping now?

Little Joanette gave me a hopeful curtsey.

'What is it, Joanette?'

'My lady,' Joanette lowered her voice to a whisper, 'could you read us the book?'

I grinned at her and nodded. Ladies didn't grin. Nor did they read the kind of book Nurse kept hidden under my mattress.

Joanette ran to fetch it. She handed it to me as if it were made of gold. But this book was more valuable than gold. All gold can do is shine. This book of stories took us to a hundred places and a thousand hearts.

It was small, with a faded cover and gilt-edged pages. I had found it in my father's library while looking for a book of French lessons to translate for Master Scholar. This book was in French, but as soon as I read the first story Nurse decided it should be hidden.

The stories were written by a woman, hundreds of years ago. Had any other woman ever written a whole book? Her name was Marie de France. A woman was remembered only if she were a queen or a saint. I could be neither. But sometimes I wished that I could do something like Marie had done, so that people would speak my name in hundreds of years' time.

I smiled at myself. What would they say? 'Ah, Juliet de Capulet — a good daughter and an obedient wife.' My mother says a woman is remembered in her children.

I opened the book. 'The Lay of Guigemar,' I translated.

'Ah,' said Nurse, 'now that is a good one. And you read it so fine, my little apple pie, just like it was proper tongue.'

In truth, I did not translate it well. I skipped the words I did not know and made up half the rest. But still, each time I read it I heard a whisper, as though from Marie herself so far away in time and place.

'Guigemar was a fair knight, the son of a king,' I said, half-reading, half-imagining. 'Straight as a spear, with strong legs and a kind smile, and hair like the glory of the sun.'

'Ah, I knew a man like that once,' said Nurse.

'One day Lord Guigemar shot an arrow at a white deer. It hit the deer, but bounced back, striking his heart too. Guigemar and the deer lay dying together on the grass. But even as she lay dying the white deer pitied him, for Guigemar's heart had not known love. In those last breaths before her death, the doe could speak too. "I must die here today. But I will give you a gift. If you can find the woman to whom your heart is joined, your arrow wound will be healed." The white doe's head dropped to the grass.'

Little Joanette stopped stitching, her eyes wide as she listened to the story. I nodded at her to keep on working.

'With his last strength, Guigemar ordered his squire to place him on an empty barge upon the river. "Let the wind and the tides carry me," he said, "until I find my love."'

'Oh, the poor gentleman,' said Nurse.

'Guigemar slept as dead on his silk pillows. The barge floated down the river to the sea. It was pushed by waves and storms. At last it came to a far land and beached itself on the sand.'

'Like one of your father's trading ships,' offered Janette.

Nurse was affronted. 'The Capulet ships sail with great skill!'

'It beached itself on the sand,' I said firmly, 'on a beach below the King's castle. His wife was young and fair. She saw the barge land, though no hand was at the sail. She and her niece hurried down over the rocks and climbed onto the barge. The Queen saw Guigemar, so fair and pale upon his cushions. She laid her hand upon his chest and found that he still lived.'

Janette pulled at a knot in her green thread. 'What was her name?'

'The book doesn't say what her name was,' I answered.

'There, what a question,' said Nurse. 'She was the Queen. What name does she need but that? A woman has her father's name, or her husband's. What needs she of another?'

I went on reading, loosely translating the words scratched on the page. 'In that one glance, that single touch, the Queen knew she loved him.'

Nurse snorted. 'One glance? What family did he have, what money? That's what you need to know before you love. Why, I remember ...'

I thought of the man beyond the mirror in my dream. How could a night shadow have a family or money? But he was a dream, no more.

'Hush,' I said to Nurse. 'Their love was so great that Guigemar was healed of his great wound. They kissed, and every day they sat together in the rose gardens of the palace.'

Janette smiled at her needle. 'Surely they did more than that. A fair man and a beautiful queen ...'

Nurse glared at her. 'You tend to your stitching. If your mistress says they sat in the gardens, that is what they did.'

'The Queen knotted Guigemar's shirt in a lover's knot that only she could untie. "I will only love a woman who can untie the knot," said Guigemar.

'Guigemar made a belt for the Queen that only he could undo. "I will never love a man unless he can untie my belt," promised the Queen.

'But the King heard of their love. He cast Guigemar back onto his barge. He hoped Guigemar would die in a shipwreck.'

'Why didn't he just kill him?' asked Joan. 'Slash him with his rapier.'

Janette shook her head. 'A king would have a sword, not a rapier. Maybe Guigemar was a swordsman like Lord Tybalt.' She blushed. 'Maybe the King was too scared to fight him.'

Somehow I didn't think Guigemar had been like Tybalt. I hoped my cousin hadn't been flirting with Janette.

'The King cast his Queen into the dungeons. The rats scratched in the darkness. Every morning, dry bread and a sponge of water were slid under her prison door. But love made her strong. She felt for the dirty sponge and drank the water. She caught mice to eat with the bread.' This was my story now. Marie de France hadn't said how the Queen survived in prison. 'Each day the Queen dreamed of Guigemar. His beauty warmed the darkness. For his sake she would not die till she had seen him again.'

The Joans had stopped their stitching. Even Nurse was silent now.

I spoke slowly, enjoying their gazes. 'For two years the Queen lay in darkness. At last she knew the King would never pardon her and she vowed to end her life. But how could she die, here in the dungeons, when she had kept living with so little for so long? And then, in a dream, it came to her. She should open the door and run to the rocks. She should cast herself down into the sea where her lover's barge had lain.

'The Queen opened her eyes and tried the door. It was unlocked! She slipped her way along the dark corridors, down through the night to the rocks. The waves crashed below the castle. But just as she was about to throw herself into the sea ...'

I paused. They looked at me, their eyes wide, even though I had told them the story before.

'... there was Guigemar's barge on the sand, just as it had been when he had first come to their shores. But this time the barge was empty. The Queen ran down to the beach and stepped aboard. The wind and waves bore her swiftly to another country — so swiftly,' I added, before Janette could ask another question, 'that she did not need food or water.

'She landed on the beach below the castle of a war-like lord, Meriaduc. He was a savage man and no woman was safe with him.'

'Like a Montague,' put in Joan.

'Most like a Montague. His legs were bandy, like a little dog's. His arms hung to his knees. His hair ...' I tried to think of something Montague-like for his hair.

'His hair was like a dirty broom,' said Nurse.

I laughed. 'That morning, the Montague had risen early to ravage the land. But when he saw the Queen on her barge he was filled with glee. He carried her back to his castle. He undid her bodice. He tried to undo her belt ...'

The Joans had almost stopped breathing now.

'... but the girdle would not untie. "What is this?" he cried.

'The Queen looked at the Montague calmly. "My belt can never be untied except by my own true love," she said. "Just as I have tied a lover's knot into his shirt."'

'Why didn't the Montague just lift her skirts?' asked Janette. Nurse silenced her with a look.

'The Montague called a great jousting tournament to try to lure the knight who could undo the Queen's belt. Every knight in the land came to compete, and Guigemar came too.

'When the Queen saw Guigemar at the banquet before the joust, she almost fainted on her bench. Guigemar saw a woman so like the one he loved. But the Queen lived in a faraway country. How could she be here?

'The Montague saw how the Queen gazed at Guigemar. He called Guigemar to the high table. The Montague said, "I have heard this knight has a knot in his shirt that no one can undo except the woman who made it. Unfasten it, so he may be free of the vow."

'The Queen's white fingers untied the knot. Guigemar kneeled on the floor. He said to the Montague, "You have saved my only love! I will be your man for three years in gratitude for what you have done."

'But the Montague only smiled. He said, "I found her, and I will keep her."'

'Oh, the evil of him,' said Nurse. 'Spoken just like a Montague.'

'Guigemar left the castle. All the knights followed him, angry at this dishonour to a lady and to love. They promised they would fight with Guigemar to free his love.

23

'They lodged that night at the castle of the Prince. The Prince welcomed them as he was at war with the Montague.'

'Ah, 'tis well to please princes,' said Nurse. 'I remember when your father —'

I spoke over her. 'The next morning, the knights rode out to take the Montague's castle. None had ever taken it before, for the walls were steep and thick. But their hearts were pure.'

'Like Lord Tybalt when he fights the Montagues,' breathed little Joanette.

I didn't think Tybalt's heart was pure.

'Time after time, they tried to scale the walls or break the drawbridge down. But the knights were beaten back. Guigemar sat on the grass within arrowshot of the keep, fasting and praying. And once again his knights stormed the castle.'

'I think Guigemar should have gone with them.' That was Janette again. 'Sitting there safe on the grass while the knights fought.'

Joanette glared at her. 'Guigemar wasn't safe. An arrow could have killed him. He was the bravest of all because he did nothing.'

I nodded. 'And by the power of Guigemar's love, the good knights won. Just like the Capulets will always beat the Montagues, because we are good and they are evil. The good knights burned the walls. They slew the

Montague in his own hall. And then Guigemar lifted his lady in his arms and bore her away to his own land. And there they lived in peace.'

'I warrant they had more than peace when they got home,' said Janette. 'Now he'd got her belt undone and all.'

Nurse stood up. 'Away with you. It's time for my lady's dinner. And there's mending to do. And chamber-pots to scrub too, if anyone deserves it,' she added darkly.

The Joans fled, though Janette was still giggling.

Nurse beamed at me. 'You said it lovely,' she said.

No bodies fell over my wall that evening as I lay on my linen pillows. Were my pillows as soft as Guigemar's? I listened to the night. The sounds of the lavender sellers and the women who sold baked apples died away. Even the yells from the tavern quietened. This was the time for peaceful sleep — or for deadly roistering. Out in the darkness, men swaggered through the streets, men in our colours or those of the Montagues, men with no purpose but to defend their own house and attack their enemies.

The Capulets were brave and noble, like the knights who fought with Guigemar. There was no lady to rescue tonight, but the Montagues had slain one of our own and cast his head into my garden. That must be avenged, just as the insults of a hundred years must be avenged, day after day ...

How had this war started? What evil had the first Montague done, so many years before? I realised I did not know. True, our houses competed for the spice trade in the city. Had the Montagues sunk one of our ships, or killed our traders? Perhaps, like Meriaduc, the Montagues were naturally bad. And bandy-legged, with hair like brooms. Rats should be swept from the streets and rooftops. So should the Montagues ...

I lay in my soft bed. Sometimes, despite the silk curtains, it seemed a prison. If only I could go to battle like a knight, or even like Tybalt. I had never seen the streets in the dark; had never walked in the street at all. I was carried in a chair to church and back, to keep my silk slippers from the mud.

One day, when I became a married woman, no longer a girl, I might walk to the market with my maids and footmen. I would go to banquets in the houses of our kin. Apart from that, my life would not change; except for Tybalt in my bed sometimes. From what I had overheard from the Joans' gossip, husbands never spent much time with their wives, just enough so they would bear children. A mistress for pleasure, a wife for heirs, and hunting or business to fill the day. I would stay living in this house, in this room, behind these walls. My mother would probably even keep the storehouse keys and instruct the housekeeper.

Out there beyond the garden wall were ... what? Brawls and adventures in the city streets. Did I want to fight the Montagues, like Tybalt? Thrust my rapier at Montague hearts, watch cockfighting and street singers, go to theatres and taverns and a hundred other places I would never see?

Master Scholar's maps showed mermaids in vast oceans, dragons in deep forests. A girl could not fight a dragon. Would I ever even see a forest, or an ocean?

Last summer, a troubadour sang to us of a maiden taming a unicorn. She braided her hair to make a rope and led it through the city.

I laughed at myself. Unicorns! My father would never allow a unicorn in his garden, nor would Tybalt when he became master here. And it would be uncomfortable to fight a dragon dressed in steel armour, and a unicorn would eat my roses.

It felt good to laugh. I remembered hearing laughter on the way to church last Sunday. I'd pushed aside the curtains of my chair to see. And there was a tavern wench, laughing, wearing a dun-coloured dress that showed her bosom, her hair straggly and undressed. It had seemed strange to me that a tavern wench could have more cause to laugh than Lord Capulet's daughter.

Was she more free than me? I thought not. Servant, wife, mother, nun, or nurse — the waves carried every woman through her life, like they had carried Guigemar's lady, who did not even have a name and was remembered only for her love.

What was love, except the dark-eyed shadow in my dream?

I felt the silk sheets on my skin. What did I want?

I did not know.

# Chapter 5

The Joans giggled as they carried in my breakfast the next morning: cherry bread today, and roast pigeons, and cold boar with sloe sauce that must have been left from my father's dinner, and the first of the year's peaches, their skin fuzzy, their cheeks flushed red, smelling of summer and sun.

I sat on my cushions and peeled a peach with a silver knife. 'What's so funny?' I asked them.

'A fight with the Montagues, my lady.' That was Joan.

I tried to give her one of my mother's stares. 'A fight with our enemies is not a joke.'

She giggled again. 'Oh, but this one was, my lady. Young Tybalt's men came up against the Montagues in the marketplace yesterday.'

'And how is that funny?'

'The whole market joined in! The man who keeps the chickens bashed the man who keeps the ducks. There were feathers everywhere! And the sheep butcher took a leg of mutton and laid into the pork butcher, who defended himself with a ham.'

'Smashed eggs everywhere,' said Janette. 'And melons slit like they were heads, and then two baker's boys took to fighting with long loaves, like they were swords.'

'The whole marketplace!' repeated Joan. 'All taking sides with the Capulets or the Montagues.'

I thought of Tybalt covered in eggs and feathers, and tried not to grin. Guigemar would never have been covered in eggs. 'I hope we won.'

Nurse pursed her lips. 'Did we win? Is that a nice question for a girl? Of course we won. Go on, girl, tell us all. Tell us how the Capulets stoned them dirty Montagues. Tell us how Lord Tybalt crushed their faces in the muck.'

'Well ...' said Janette slowly.

Surely we had not lost! I stared at the Joans. 'What aren't you telling me?'

'Lord Montague was in the market too,' said Joan, the smile gone now. 'And so was your father, and your lady mother. And your father drew his sword and rushed at Lord Montague.'

'My father? Fighting!' I put down my slice of peach. My father was an old man, nearly forty-five. I hardly knew him — between his warehouse and his mistress he had little time for a daughter — but he was the head of our house. 'Was he hurt?'

30

'Hurt? Your father! Oh, your father could stop a thousand Montagues!' said Nurse.

'Your lady mother held him back,' said Joan. 'And Lady Montague her husband too. And then the Prince's men rode in, and then the Prince himself.'

Had the Prince and his men joined the fight on our side? Surely then it had become a proper battle, not a marketplace brawl.

'And then?' I demanded.

'Then nothing, my lady. The Prince stopped the fight.'

'He did not order the Montagues back to their kennels, with their dogs?'

'No, my lady.'

I trembled as I wiped off the peach juice. How could the Prince not see what rats the Montagues were?

Joan added quietly, her eyes downcast, 'The Prince says there are to be no more battles in his city.'

I tried to keep the anger from my voice. A nice girl never showed her anger. 'Even the Prince's word cannot chain Tybalt. Capulets and Montagues have always fought. They will not stop now.'

The Joans had lost their giggles.

'They will have to,' said Janette quietly. 'The Prince ordered your lord father and Lord Montague to his castle to speak privately with them. There was a proclamation in the marketplace, and along the streets too. Any Montague or Capulet who fights will be put to death.'

I sat silent. Death for fighting in the streets? Men had always fought. They always would. The Montagues deserved to die! And yet ... A battle with a leg of lamb against a leg of pork was not a brave knight's quest. I stared out at the garden while the Joans and Nurse finished my breakfast.

Nurse was chewing the last pigeon when a footman pushed aside the door curtains. He bowed. 'Master Scholar is come.'

'What, already!' Nurse said. The Joans bustled away the cloth and dishes.

Master Scholar made me a stiff bow, looking down his nose like a grey peacock, all thin shanks and long nose and dusty black clothes from fifty years ago. He even wore a codpiece. I had giggled when I first saw it, till Nurse frowned at me.

'Good morrow, Lady Juliet. How goes your French translation?'

My French translation? It was under the cushion where I had shoved it.

I looked innocently at Nurse. 'Have you seen my French translation?'

Nurse clicked her fingers at Master Scholar. 'French? Who would speak French?'

He glared. 'The French, and anyone who would call herself a lady.'

Nurse snorted. 'Is my chicken not a lady born? The

whole world knows that if you fill a lady's head with too much learning you will send her mad. And besides, she was translating like a lark for us just yesterday, like she was French born, or better, for I am sure they have no Capulets in France.'

Master Scholar ignored her. 'Your pages of translation, Lady Juliet.'

I sighed. Master Scholar did his duty to my father, and I must do mine. I reached under the cushion as the footman pushed through the curtains again.

'Her ladyship would have her daughter come.'

It had been weeks since my mother had called for me. Last time, we had made sugar sweetmeats in her still room, mixing almonds and white sugar into marzipan coloured with spinach juice to make small trees, and moulding small sugar cups that looked like tiny roses. It was a lesson only a mother could give her daughter, for sugar is too expensive to trust to servants, even in a house as rich as ours. Perhaps today we'd preserve cherries …

I tried not to grin. 'Your pardon, Master Scholar.'

'No, your mother's will be done.'

He looked as relieved as I did. Poor Master Scholar. I hoped his other students were more eager.

Nurse wiped the pigeon grease off her chin and gestured to the Joans. 'Straighten your lady's coif. See that her hands are clean.'

I lifted them to show her I had not got ink on them yet. I had not even lifted up my quill. You would think ink loved me more than any in the land, it stuck to my fingers so.

Nurse fussed at my hair as we followed the footman along the portrait gallery under the gazes of my grandfathers and uncles and great-uncles: the one who went on a crusade, the one stabbed by a Montague, the one who was a bishop, and the one who had first sent our ships as far as the Spice Islands. The Montagues had never dared to venture there until we Capulets had led the way.

Down the stairs, Nurse lifting my skirts, along the hall with its tall stained-glass windows, then out to the stone terrace above the rose garden. My mother stood there, pointing out the blooms she wanted cut. Her fair hair showed a few threads of grey on either side of her coif.

Nurse curtseyed. 'Madam, she is here.'

My mother turned and assessed me in the way I supposed all mothers did. My dress and posture I could correct, but nothing could make me tall or fair like her. My mother seemed always to judge me by what I was not, not what I was. I was not a son. Nor was I a beauty, as she had been, with hair a field of gold.

I gave her my best curtsey, a swift sweep down then up. To my surprise she smiled at me, then looked at Nurse. 'Nurse, you know my daughter's of a pretty age ...'

Nurse curtseyed and talked at the same time. 'She was born on the same night as our Susan, God rest her soul ...'

Nurse's own baby had died, which had left her with milk for me. I concentrated on smiling politely. Down at the end of the garden servants carried chairs into the banquet hall. Cooks lugged linen-covered trays. My parents must be holding a banquet this afternoon.

'... she was the prettiest babe ever I nursed and I might live to see her married ...'

My mother held up her hand. 'Marry, that marry is the very theme I came to talk of.' She turned to me and smiled again. 'Tell me, daughter Juliet, how comes your disposition to be married?'

Married? At thirteen! Tybalt must be in debt, I thought. He needs my dowry to pay his bills.

'It is an honour I dream not of,' I told my mother.

I lied. Of course I lied. I had dreamed of marriage every night since I was four years old. Marriage to a knight like Guigemar; to the dark shadow in my dream, who would love me till the sun crumbled like yellow cheese, a love so strong that poets wrote of it.

I never dreamed of marriage to Tybalt. I knew it was necessary, but I was in no hurry for it to happen. Tybalt was ... Suddenly I had the word. A peacock, parading his honour to the world, all feathers with little meat behind.

But why was my mother talking of marriage now? She could lend Tybalt money if he needed it. A daughter could be five and twenty and still not wed, especially if the marriage was a settled thing. But a nice girl does not ask her mother questions. I bit my lip.

My mother waited just long enough to make sure I would not ask. 'The valiant Paris seeks you for his love.'

Who was Paris? Had there been a miracle? Had a knight spied me in church? That was the only place I ever showed my face beyond these walls. Was Paris my shadow lover, come to claim me?

My mother watched me, still smiling. For a moment it was as though she was truly happy for me — me, a person, not just the girl who was her daughter.

'Verona's summer hath not such a flower,' she said softly. 'The Earl of Paris is cousin to the Prince.'

So that was why she smiled. The Prince's cousin wanted to marry me! An earl, not just a wealthy trader like the Capulets. For the first time I had done something that made my mother proud. Our family joined to the Prince's? I put up my chin. Let the Montagues match that!

Nurse clapped her hands. 'Cousin to the Prince! He's a flower, in faith, a very flower!'

My mother took a rose from the footman and smelled it thoughtfully. 'What say you? Can you love the gentleman? Today you shall behold him at our feast.'

So this was the cause of the banquet. The Earl of Paris had come to woo me! I would have a household of my own, a grand one. I would wear the household keys. No Master Scholar. No French translation ever again. A husband who was cousin to the Prince …

My mother went on and on, talking of Paris's virtues, which gave me time to work out a polite way to answer. My tongue would never have the poetry of my mother's. Though as the wife of the Earl of Paris I would try to learn. A lady must speak in poetry, especially in the royal family.

Royal! A banquet today! What would I wear? I had never even appeared in company before.

At last my mother came to a halt, just as I had worked out something proper to say.

'I'll look to like, if looking liking move. But no more deep will I endart mine eye than your consent gives strength to make it fly.'

A good speech, dutiful, poetic. It even rhymed.

My mother smiled, the best smile she had ever given me, and gave me her hand to kiss.

# Chapter 6

I danced back along the corridor. Well, no, I didn't. Young ladies only danced when the minstrel played, and never along a corridor. I walked behind Nurse, eyes downwards, till a pair of red velvet shoes made me look up.

Red shoes, red stockings, red breeches, and above them Tybalt's face, with a black eye and an expression that was hard to read. His wolfhound gave a faint whine beside him.

'Fair cousin, a flower soon to bloom, I hear.'

Tybalt bent down and gave me a kiss of greeting on the lips. I could taste his anger, bitter as old rye bread. My mother must have told him about the marriage before she had told me. Tybalt had lost the whole House of Capulet today, and must pretend it didn't matter. The Earl of Paris would be my father's heir now.

I looked at him nervously. His anger glittered, but he had it in check. Tybalt needed my mother's goodwill more than ever now. He would even need mine, I thought, when I was married to the Earl of Paris. My husband would hold the keys to the House of Capulet after my father's death.

Tybalt forced a smile. I felt sorry for him; sorry for the whole world who wasn't Juliet Capulet today. 'I wish you hadn't had to hear this news, cousin.'

'Sorry enough to say "nay" to a noble husband?' I could see the effort behind his gallantry. 'No need to frown, my gentle cousin. You are the gift of your good father.'

The wolfhound barked sharply, as though he knew that something wasn't right. Tybalt ignored him and kissed my hand.

'There,' he said, 'if I have not your hand in marriage, at least I have kissed it. Will you dance with me at the banquet this afternoon, kind cousin?'

'Yes, sir, I'll gladly dance with you.' I tried to make him smile. 'I like the new adornment for your eye, cousin.'

He almost managed a grin. 'A gift from the Montagues.'

'I hope you gave them presents in return.'

He laughed. 'I did. So did your father! Your mother had to hold him back. In truth, it were more a brawl than a fight for gentlemen. I even saw one of the Montague rats felled by a well-thrown cabbage.' His grin was real now, as he touched his eye. 'That may be how I got this.'

'A cabbage is a fit weapon to slay a Montague. I hope my father gets to wield his sword next time.'

Tybalt shook his head. 'The Prince has ordered torture and death to any Capulet or Montague who fights again.'

So the Joans had been right. 'Does the Prince wish peace so much?'

Tybalt's hand fondled the head of his rapier. 'A peaceful city means prosperous trade. Prosperous trade means more riches.'

It sounded sensible, not romantic. But a battle with cabbages wasn't romance either. And a prince must always be right. For the first time I wondered if the Prince saw our families as squabbling children, quarrelling together as my brother and I had about who would ride the rocking horse. I am grown up today, I thought, and Tybalt is still a boy.

'Will the Prince really put anyone who fights to death?' I asked.

'Yes.' Tybalt lifted his rapier from its scabbard. It shone in the sun from the window. He lunged, so suddenly his dog barked, then laughed as he put the rapier back. It was not a pleasant laugh. 'I must exercise with shadow Montagues instead of their rat-like hides.'

I smiled, as he had meant me to. It was easy to smile this morning. The Prince was right. Peace was better than battles with cabbages, than severed heads thrown into gardens. I would be nobility, above squabbles in the alleys and marketplace. My son would be an earl one day, as well as head of the House of Capulet, far above any Montague! But I hoped my father had promised Tybalt that he would always be a valued member of our house. Today I hoped the whole world could be happy.

Nurse pulled my hand. 'Come on, my dearie. It will take two hours to get you ready, though indeed I've had your betrothal dress ready these two years ... The flies will get the banquet first if we don't hurry.'

Tybalt bowed. I walked away with Nurse, then stopped. My lovebird lay in the corridor, its neck snapped.

Nurse whistled for a footman, who carried the small corpse away. He said nothing. Nor did Nurse, or not about the bird.

I stood while the Joans stripped my clothes off me and washed me again. The new shift they slipped over my head was silk, not linen. Over it went a corset to nip in my waist, then a hoop skirt of arched whalebone, and a yellow silk petticoat. The Joans sewed on the yellow sleeves, then fastened a jewelled stomacher on an overgown of red velvet and scarlet lace. More stitching now, for slashed oversleeves to show the yellow underneath, and then still more sleeves, slashed even more and embroidered with pearls, and a half-ruff of white, sewn about my neck.

My feet ached from standing still while they worked on me. I had never seen these clothes before. My mother must have ordered them for just such a day.

Nurse arranged my mother's pearls in three strands around my neck and bosom; then pearl rings and earrings and another strand about my waist. It took hours to dress as a lady should for company, and at least five hundred pins and stitches. Today it seemed there were two thousand.

Now they worked on my hair, brushing it with rose oil to make it shine, curling tongs at the front, and then a French net, with pearls too. Then they began on my face: red wax on my lips, kohl about my eyes, making a Juliet fit to be the Earl of Paris's bride.

The Earl of Paris! Could I love him, as my mother had asked? Had the Earl of Paris fallen in love with me, like Guigemar had with the Queen?

I shook my head. What was love, except the duty one owed one's parents and one's husband? Dreams were just that: shadows of the night.

No, I would have a noble husband, and a household of my own. My father would not choose a cruel man for me, nor a stupid one to inherit his estates. I would be well contented with his choice. To be mistress of my own home! My mother would find me a trustworthy steward; I would have my household running like oiled silk. Nurse would come with me, of course, and the Joans. I glanced at them. They were as flushed as if my good fortune was theirs too — which in many ways it was.

'There you are,' said Nurse, 'as fair as a singing bird. Though to be sure a singing bird is not always fair. I saw one once that had lost quite half his feathers …'

I kissed her to shut her up, then lifted my skirts to run along the gallery, not wanting to be late. Nurse followed me to the terrace, then stopped.

I turned to her. I had never in my life gone anywhere without my nurse. She smiled at me, and brushed at a tear. For once her flood of words had vanished.

'Go on, my little lamb,' she whispered. 'You will be a woman now.'

I lifted up my skirts again and crossed the terrace, my head high, feeling the pebbles of the path under my slippers. I walked alone along the gravel path through the rose bushes, towards the banquet hall.

# Chapter 7

Ours is a good hall. My brother and I played there when we were small, hiding behind the tapestries while Nurse looked on. He had been four years old that day, two months before he caught the flux, and I was six. The hall had been all shadows. Now its shutters were open and light poured in, like golden wine. A horseshoe of tables half-filled the banquet room, covered with white linen, and set with silver forks and spoons, goblets of Venetian glass, trenchers and linen napkins. The glasses of jellies and sweetmeats were laid out already; and small sugar cupids pulled their arrows at each setting, with marzipan hearts and roses. My father's chair, with its arched back and arms, stood at the centre of the main table. My mother's had been placed next to his, smaller, low-backed and armless; and next to hers stood a chair as grand as my father's, for the Earl of Paris.

I was early. I sat in the waiting room behind the banquet hall, my hands in my lap. I heard the guests arrive: cousins and second cousins, known to me since I was small and allowed to join the adults for an hour at Christmas-tide and on saints' days. I heard Tybalt's voice, laughing a little too loudly.

I felt sweat drip down my neck, smelling of the rosewater I'd been washed with. I realised I was scared. What would the Earl be like? What should I say to him? He would be dignified, close to my father's age. I should have rehearsed something, all the poetic words fitting for a well-bred young lady. Instead, I felt as dumb as a lovebird in a cage that has not been taught to talk.

I thought of my bird, dead on the floor.

The door opened and my father strode in. 'Well, my daughter?'

He smelled of wine and lavender and bearskin. I curtseyed. My mother's face was a smooth mask of white lead, her cheeks and lips rouged like the rubies at her throat and ears. Her hand rested on the jewelled and velvet-clad arm of a stranger. I curtseyed more deeply, too deeply to see the stranger's face.

'My Lord Paris, may I present my daughter?' I had never heard my father so pleased before.

I rose and looked at the man I was to marry. He was tall. He might have been Verona's flower, as my mother had promised. He was also a boy, sixteen perhaps. He still had pimples on his chin.

How could this boy be a friend of my father? Because he is a prince's cousin, I thought. Because he is an earl.

I hoped I had not gaped at him. He wore red silk stockings on fine legs and a gold velvet doublet embroidered with silver. Only those of noble blood may wear gold or silver. The eagle feather in his tall hat was gilded. If Tybalt was a peacock, then this boy was a rooster. He knew that he was the noble here, that he did our house an honour in asking for my hand. All his gold and silver shouted it aloud.

The Earl of Paris swept off his hat. He bowed as deeply as if I were royalty. 'My honoured lady.'

I caught my mother's eye, then quickly held out my hand so the Earl could kiss the air above it.

'My loving daughter, Lord Paris, our house's blooming rose, my Juliet.' My mother's speech was as perfect as always.

The silence grew. I had to say something. All poetry had flown. 'Yes, I am Juliet,' I said, then wished the tapestries would fall and cover me.

The young Earl laughed, as if he were pleased I hadn't a too-ready wit. 'A rose indeed,' he said. 'And with no thorns, or sharp tongue to bite.'

He bent and kissed my lips in greeting. His breath smelled of caraway. He held out his arm to me and I slipped my hand onto his sleeve. The musicians began to play. My father led my mother into the hall. The Earl of Paris and I followed.

I sat on the bench next to the Earl. The table's centrepiece was a forest made out of marzipan, covered with a snow of sugar and ice. The snow had begun to melt in the heat of the fire and many people, revealing summer-green sugar trees beneath it.

Servants brought in the first course: a suckling pig with an apple in its mouth; turkeys with their feathers painted on; a haunch of venison with turnips; two lambs, dressed whole with salad, on a bed of roses made of carved radishes.

The horns blew. The harpists played. Tybalt laughed too loudly again farther down the table. Once he would have sat between my mother and myself. Not now.

Servants served the wine from the sideboard. The young Earl helped me to slices of pig, to venison, his manners perfect. Too perfect. My father had once bidden actors to come to his name-day feast to perform for our family and cousins. This boy was like an actor, playing the lover, showing everyone how an earl could be gracious to a family that traded for its wealth.

This was no wooing. There were no words of love. This boy in his cloth of gold was not Guigemar. I knew why he had offered for me. If there was love at this table, it was for my father's estates, the wealth from his ships.

I drank the wine, then wished I hadn't. The table was already too bright, too loud. I had never drunk unwatered wine before.

The dishes were removed; the second course brought in. A tall pile of fried larks; leeks in honey; cheese pies; a loin of veal with pomegranate seeds; gilt-edged pies cut open to show hare and chicken in gold jelly with hard-boiled eggs; fat capons stuffed with rice coloured gold with saffron. Gold food, to match the Earl's gold clothes.

I ate, I drank.

The young Earl talked to my mother about his country estate, in between helping me to food I did not want. His house had been built by his great-grandfather; it had pools of carp, a thousand glass windows, fountains in a grotto ... A boasting boy. One day the carp pools and fountains would be mine, but I would not boast.

The servants brought in the final course. I was glad there were only three courses today. My mother looked more intent as they carried in the new dishes, for they were the work of her and her ladies. I too had helped make those trees and sugar cups. I remembered the disgrace when I had burned the sugar when I was seven years old. It had been a fortnight before my mother had called for me again.

The servants put the centrepiece in front of the Earl. There was a marzipan forest with a tiny marzipan knight killing a boar, just like the knight and boar on the Earl of Paris's crest. The wafers had the Earl's crest on them too. The apple pastries were in the shape of a child in a cradle. The rose cups were filled with stewed quinces, the food of love.

A cooing from the second cousins. My cheeks flushed. It would have been less obvious if my mother had hired a town crier to yell it through the streets: 'My daughter and the Prince's kinsman are to be wed!'

'My lady?' The Earl of Paris smiled at me and offered me the sugar knight. I saw that he chewed his fingernails. 'Will you take my knight?' He bent and added too loudly in my ear, 'This knight, and all the nights to come.'

I felt my cheeks turn as red as my dress. I took the knight, already a little sticky from his fingers. 'I thank you, sir. I will indeed accept your knight.'

'Which part will you eat first?'

I flushed with anger. I hoped he would take it for modesty. 'Why, sir, he is too fine. I will keep him to admire.'

My mother nodded almost imperceptibly at my answer.

'By your bed?' He looked around the table, expecting everyone to applaud his wit.

'Nay, sir, I would not keep him so confined. By the window, so he can look down upon the town.'

And where, hopefully, a sparrow would eat him before breakfast tomorrow.

The Earl had not noticed the bite in my voice. 'A good wife's answer, not to keep her lord confined.'

'As she is a good daughter, she will be a good wife,' my mother said.

Her voice was quiet, but there was a hint of steel too. She didn't like this boy teasing me. I wondered if perhaps she loved me, not just as her daughter but the me inside. Our eyes met briefly, then she turned to the Earl of Paris with a smile.

Shadows grew outside. The lamps were lit in the gardens, bringing the last of the day's scent of roses. The table's grand centrepiece had melted from winter to summer, adorned with marzipan wheat and apples for fingers to pluck.

More guests arrived to dance, masked as bears, as stags, as birds. My father laughed and donned a mask too. So did some of the cousins. But I did not, nor did my mother or the Earl of Paris.

The musicians played. My hand touched the Earl's in the dance before he passed on; his skin was soft. We met again as the dance came to its close. The Earl bowed to me, then went over to the musicians. They stopped playing to attend to him. The dancers waited for the music to begin for the next set.

The musicians took up their instruments again. A drum beat softly. Lord Paris began to sing. His voice was still high, not quite a man's, but well trained.

*My mistress's eyes are like the sun,*
*Her lips are red as coral,*
*If snow be white, her breasts be snow,*
*And I the fortunate to know,*
*Her rose is plucked by only one*
*Who'll ever wear her laurel.*

I thought: he should be singing a love song to me. Instead, he was singing a song to the company, claiming me and the House of Capulet, while my father smiled among them.

The music stopped, to laughter and applause. The Earl of Paris bowed, as dignified as if he were forty years old, then turned to speak to my father. The servants poured them wine.

'Well, can you love him?' My mother spoke softly.

I met her eyes again. 'With a daughter's duty, and a wife's.'

She nodded, satisfied. 'Do not confuse a poet's love with that found between a husband and his wife. My dear, he will not use you ill. Better to come to him rich with the dowry of a wealthy house and fine estates. Respect lives on when love has died.'

My mother spoke from experience. She had brought two large estates to my father when they married.

She touched my cheek gently. 'If you give him heirs, my dear, and a great estate, he will be happy. If he is happy, you shall be too.'

'And if ... if there are no heirs?'

'A rich dowry can be a great comfort to a man.' Her voice was dry. My mother had not succeeded in giving my father an heir who had reached manhood. 'The Earl will guard our house well. That too is important.'

I watched my intended husband laugh with my father. There would be no courtship then; no suitors vying for my love like in the stories. I would exchange my father's house for my husband's, with a prince for a cousin, my husband's bed instead of French lessons, children, and the respect of the city as the Earl's wife. And from the day I married, the House of Capulet would be a noble one, leaving the rats of Montague scrabbling in the marketplace muck.

Guigemar existed only in a book. This was real. What else could I want?

# Chapter 8

'Love,' sang the minstrel. He stroked his mandolin.

> *Love in the month of maying,*
> *When merry lads are playing, fa la,*
> *Each with his bonny lass*
> *Upon the greeny grass.*
> *Fa la la! Fa la lala, la la.*
>
> *The Spring, clad all in gladness,*
> *Doth laugh at Winter's sadness, fa la,*
> *And to the bagpipe's sound*
> *The lovers tread out their ground.*
> *Fa la la! Fa la lala, la la.*

I joined the dance, one hand linked to the other dancers, the other holding up my skirts. It was a dance I had performed a hundred times with the Joans and my dance master, but it was different here, dancing with strangers by torchlight. This was my home. But it was also another world, the world of womanhood.

I liked it not. Womanhood seemed like the dance, with steps that no dancer was allowed to change. I would be my father's daughter and my husband's wife. But Juliet, who was she? A person as insubstantial as our shadows on the wall.

The guests had all stared at me a short time ago. I had been like the table centrepiece when it was fresh upon the table. Now my snow had melted. The guests laughed with one another, watched the dancers or joined in. My mother had moved down to the terrace. Even the Earl of Paris was back in the banqueting room, discussing I knew not what with men my father's age. No one even glanced at me.

Except for one. Even through the room's warmth I felt the heat of someone's gaze. I searched the crowd to find his face as I wove in and out inside the dance.

And then I saw him. He stood by the pillar on the terrace, slightly beyond the flaring light of the torches. I knew him. I had known him all my life. He was my dream shadow, come to life.

He wasn't tall; not much taller, perhaps, than I. He wasn't handsome. A little plump, like me. Brown hair. Brown eyes that smiled. Young — Tybalt's age perhaps. But Tybalt was a boy, and the Earl a boy too, despite his conversations with the older men. This was a man.

He had been wearing a mask; I saw it dangling by

his waist. I did not need to see the rapier by his side to know he was a gentleman. He bore himself as one of noble blood. Rings on his fingers, but no other jewels; no peacock displaying himself. His eyes held mine, straight and true. We knew each other for a hundred years in that one glance. He looked at me with love. I had only ever seen love in my dreams, but I knew it now as if I had met it a thousand times.

I hadn't danced with him. His hand would have burned mine if once we had touched. If our bodies had brushed against each other ...

I stopped dancing so suddenly that the ladies either side had to remind me to move on. I lifted my hands again and made the right steps. I had never felt my body properly before. It was something others tended, something to be fed and washed and dressed. Now I felt every part of my skin. My body was a star. No, half a star. The other half was him.

The dance ended. I curtseyed. No one looked at me, except for him. His gaze burned through the crowd. So, I thought, this is what it is to be a woman.

The minstrels began another song. I stepped from the dance floor as a yell shattered the music. 'Fetch me my rapier!'

I looked back to see Tybalt pulling at a servant's shoulder. He'd had too much to drink. Too much of everything, perhaps, today.

My father stepped in quickly to quieten him. 'Why, how now, kinsman, wherefore you storm so?'

Tybalt gazed wildly about the room. 'Uncle! There is a Montague at your banquet! Now by the honour of my kin, I'll strike him dead, and hold it not a sin.'

The guests all stared at Tybalt. No, not all. I glanced back at the young man to see his eyes still on me.

I looked back at my cousin. His hands shook with anger as he snatched his rapier from a footman. The room grew silent under the beat of music. For certain, Tybalt had drunk too much wine. How could a Montague dare to come here, to pollute our walls? Poor Tybalt. He had lost the House of Capulet today. Now he was being a fool, in front of all our guests.

My father smiled, and shook his head at us, as though to say, 'It is nothing.' He drew Tybalt into a corner. Tybalt's face was flushed, his rapier still in his hand, but the ripple his anger had caused died away and the guests began to dance again.

I looked at the young man by the pillar once more. I watched him watching me. Vaguely I was aware of Tybalt striding through the room, flinging his mask down at the door. Then he was gone. I didn't care.

Another dance began, but I stood back. Silks and velvets, damask and lace, dancers and musicians ... it was as if they were a painted backdrop for the young man and me. If a man's life can be contained in a book, then his face was a book too. I could read his life there, just as I had read the Earl's.

But there was no Earl now. There was no one except us two. Could I reach him? Perhaps, even now, if I walked to him, I would find a sheet of glass between us. Perhaps he would merge with the shadows and be a dream.

He did not walk towards me. He let me come to him. No one had given me that gift of choice before.

I moved slowly around the room, nodding at an uncle, kissing a cousin on her lips. Out onto the terrace, past the fall of light. He stood there, still, and watched me come. I was almost near enough to feel his warmth.

I stopped, suddenly unsure. What should I say? I had never greeted a gentleman without my mother or my father to introduce us. Should I curtsey? And yet it was as if we had known each other from the moment of our births. I held out my hand for him to kiss, as my mother did to men whom she knew well.

He did not kiss my hand. He took my fingers, then matched his hand to mine. The world changed in that single touch.

He did not smile. Nor did I.

He spoke softly, so only I could hear. 'If I profane with my unworthiest hand this holy shrine, the gentle fine is this: my lips, two blushing pilgrims, ready stand to smooth that rough touch with a tender kiss.'

It was a question. To kiss, or not to kiss? Once more, he left me to decide. I felt my smile grow. The poetry I had not been able to find for Paris came easily now.

I glanced at our hands, already kissing. 'Good pilgrim, you do wrong your hand too much. For saints have hands that pilgrims' hands do touch, and palm to palm is holy palmers' kiss.'

He moved so close that I could smell his breath. He smelled of a garden in summer, the moment the earth gives its blessing for the plants to grow. 'Have not saints lips, and holy palmers too?'

My smile became a grin. I was Juliet now, and not my mother's daughter. 'Ay, pilgrim, lips that they must use in prayer.'

His eyes crinkled with the joke. 'Oh, then, dear saint, let lips do what hands do. Move not while my prayer's effect I take. Thus from my lips, by yours, my sin is purged.'

His lips met mine. To anyone watching it would have seemed a cousin's kiss. But I had kissed many cousins, and none like this. We were awkward at first; I did not know where to put my nose. And then our lips met properly. The kiss lasted a scatter of drops from the fountain. It lasted half my life.

He drew back, his eyes on mine.

'Then have my lips the sin that they have took,' I said. This time I kissed him.

His hand tightened on mine. 'Sin from thy lips? Oh trespass sweetly urged! Give me my sin again.'

I pressed my body to him. Our lips met …

'Madam, your mother craves a word with you.'

It was Nurse. She must have been watching from the servants' door. I flushed and dropped him a curtsey. My hand felt suddenly bereft, as did my lips.

Nurse gave me a warning stare as we made our way back to the dancing. I turned to smile at him and caught his smile at me. It warmed me as his lips had done, a warmth that flowed through my body like a rose unfurling.


My mother was talking to her aunt, who wore the same green she had worn to the last Christmas feast, and the one before. Her wrinkles sagged into her wimple.

I curtseyed to her, then to my mother. 'Madam, you wished for me?'

'Dear child, many times have I wished for such a daughter, and I have her now. But I did not call for you.' She patted my cheek. 'We shall see a betrothal ring this summer.'

I blushed and nodded, then realised my mother spoke of Paris. The banquet seemed a hundred miles away. So did the Earl of Paris. I could never marry the Earl now. What would my mother say when I refused him? What would my father think of his daughter choosing a man to love?

I met my mother's gaze. She looked happy for me; happy that I was happy, not merely because I was to marry a kinsman of the Prince. Perhaps if I chose another, she would accept my choice.

And my father? I did not know my lover's name, but the rubies on his fingers, his fashionable rapier and his bearing told me he was wealthy. He must be of a good house to be here tonight. He might not be an earl, but surely my father would like him well enough to let him court me.

Suddenly I realised I did not even know if he lived here in Verona. Was he a visitor?

It didn't matter. Even if he were a stranger, anyone here could tell him who I was. He would come to our house tomorrow, to seek my father's leave to court me. My father would find out his family and estate. Perhaps he even had royal connections, like the Earl …

I turned to look at him. But no dark-eyed man gazed at me from the terrace.

Where was he? Had he gone to find someone to introduce us?

I moved through the crowd. He had vanished. Gone, just like my dreams. But he was not a dream. I could still feel his warmth on my lips, my hand.

And then I saw him. He stood by the door to the street, with two young men I did not know.

He was going! And not even a farewell to me! Had

I imagined all we had exchanged? No. Then why was he leaving?

My breath hurt suddenly, as though my heart clenched too hard around it. I had to find out his name, at least, before he left. I slipped over to the servants' door and hissed: 'Nurse!'

She peered out, holding a goblet of wine, her fingers sticky with date pastry. 'What is it, my lamblet?'

'Who is that young gentleman?'

Nurse looked over to the door. 'The one with the silver stocking tops? That's the son and heir of old Tiberio.'

'Who is he that now is going out the door?'

'With the eagle plume in his hat? Young Petrucio.'

'No! The man who follows him, who didn't dance?'

Nurse shrugged and grabbed another pastry from a passing tray. 'I know not.'

'Go, ask his name,' I told her. 'If he be married, my grave is like to be my wedding bed.'

She looked at me, alarmed. 'What do you mean?'

'Go!'

Someone touched my arm: a cousin, to ask if I would dance the next set. I shook my head. When I looked back to the door, the three young men had gone. He would come back! He had to. He was seeing his friends to their chairs ...

Nurse made her way through the crowd towards me. She looked as grim as when Joanette had spilled orange juice on my new gown. No, worse. She pulled me into the shadows.

'His name is Romeo, and a Montague; the only son of your great enemy.'

He could not be a Montague. If he were a Montague, then everything I knew was wrong. A Montague was evil, vile.

The world cracked open. The noises were too loud, the fire too hot.

'My only love sprung from my only hate!' I whispered. 'Too early seen unknown, and known too late! Prodigious birth of love it is to me, that I must love a loathed enemy.'

Nurse stared at me. 'What's this?'

If he were a Montague, then all I had believed was wrong. The world swam, as though every candle flickered at the same time. Even the firelight seemed not quite real.

I would not sob. I would not show my anguish on my face. I said, 'A rhyme I learned from someone I danced with.'

It was not a lie. For we had danced our own dance, there in the shadows, he and I.

'Juliet!'

It was my mother's voice, from inside the banquet room. Most of the guests had moved there now. Supper would be served. I had to sit with her, and the Earl of Paris. I had to smile. Tybalt was trained for fighting. I had been trained for this.

I smiled. My fingernails dug into my clenched hands. 'Anon!' I called to my mother.

Nurse looked at me, concerned. 'Come,' she said, 'let's away. The strangers are all gone.'

Gone? He would never be gone from my heart. But he was a Montague.

How could a Capulet love a Montague? Who was Juliet if not the dutiful daughter who loved and hated where she was told?

I stepped away from Nurse, towards supper in the banquet room.

# Chapter 9

The guests had left. I walked with my mother along the gravel path back to the house. My face and heart ached from smiling.

The moon shone, brighter than the lamps. The day's fragrance hung in puddles under the rose bushes. Was it only a few hours since I had walked this way? I was a girl then. I was a woman now. Love had been a word to me, a dream. Love was not for Juliet Capulet. Now it was life itself. He was a Montague ...

We stepped up onto the terrace and into the house. It smelled of the bowls of dried oranges and cloves. Dishes clanked, over in the kitchens. My mother stopped at the staircase and kissed my forehead. 'A good beginning,' she said quietly. 'Your father is well pleased, and so is Paris. And you?'

'I ... I know not what I feel.'

She looked amused. 'Quite proper. Goodnight, my dear.'

Her women were waiting for her at the top of the stairs. Nurse waited with the Joans for me. I led them along the corridor to my room, let them undress me, unpick the stitches, take the clothes away, undo my hair and brush it, then plait it for the night, clean my face with rosewater, and dress me in my nightshift. Janette drew the warming pan across the sheets. I lay down obediently, and let them pull the covers over me.

Nurse lay in the truckle bed, her snores like a mob of bulls going to the market.

I could not sleep. Before tonight I had been content with dreams. Not now.

I lay there as the shadows of the garden played with the moonbeams on my walls. I tried to think. My mind was too full, too weary from the long day and night. Had there ever been a day so long as this?

His name was Romeo. He was a Montague.

Why had he come to a Capulet feast? Was he the Montague Tybalt had spied? Was that why Tybalt had stormed from the hall? But if my father had known there was a Montague in his banquet hall, why had he not had him thrown out?

Perhaps my father knew that everyone who wore the name Montague wasn't evil. Was the hatred between our houses one of the games that adults played? My mother pretended that my father had no mistress. When I was six years old, I had seen her ignore the madman who bared his buttocks in the marketplace. I had laughed, till my mother told me, 'Nice girls do not see such things,' as if it were my fault for looking, and not his for showing.

For some reason, our two families played the game of hatred. But hatred killed. Suddenly all the years of hatred slid away and I could think again. I would play my parents' game no longer. I was not the daughter they had tried to make, like the sugar cups my mother had made for the feast. The sugar cups had dissolved. I had dissolved too. The good daughter had vanished, leaving only me.

Romeo ...

I had heard the name before. A cousin had once said, 'Romeo is a good lad,' then added hurriedly, 'For a Montague.' Tybalt had sneered and said, 'A rat is still a rat.'

More important was what I had not heard. Tybalt had never boasted of fighting with Romeo Montague. No one had ever laughed at the heir of Montague lying drunk in the street, or brawling by the city gates. If there had been bad to tell, someone would have told it, so we could all laugh at the Montagues.

Nothing bad, and something good ...

Perhaps, if his name were not Montague, Romeo might have been the man my father chose for me, the heir of a house like ours.

I could not marry the Earl of Paris now. My loyalty to Capulet had vanished with the torchlight. My family had played me like a chess piece. They cared for me no more than a piece in their games. Now I was myself, not theirs. Just Juliet.

The moonlight danced along the balcony. I slipped from my bed, the rush matting cold under my feet. I stepped onto the balcony and pulled the curtain behind me. I gazed across the garden at the sleeping town, the last curls of smoke drifting up towards the sky. The breeze whispered against my bare arms. *Love*, it murmured, *love*.

Was Romeo sleeping somewhere out there? How could two names keep us apart?

'Romeo.' It was the first time I had said his name aloud. I spoke to the garden, to the sky. 'Romeo ... give up your name. Or if you'll be my love, then I'll no longer be a Capulet. It is only your name that is my enemy. Oh, be some other name! What's in a name? That which we call a rose would smell as sweet with any other name. Throw away your name, and for that name, take all myself.'

A laugh below me. 'I take thee at thy word.'

'What?' I stumbled back. 'Who are you?'

For a moment I wondered if I were asleep. This was my dream: the rose garden, the shadows, the voice of my love ... I had dreamed this a thousand times ...

Then my heart grew steady. Even before he spoke, I knew. He was himself, and I was myself, and we were real, and now.

Romeo stepped forward from the shade of a rose bush. How long had he been standing there, listening, watching?

'I know not how to tell you who I am,' he said. 'My name, dear saint, is hateful to myself, because it is an enemy to you.'

'Are you not Romeo and a Montague?' I whispered.

'Neither, fair saint, if either you dislike.'

I leaned over the balcony, my heart beating with terror for him. What if a servant heard us and let out the dogs? Or Tybalt appeared with his rapier? 'The place is death, considering who you are, if any of my kinsmen find you here. If they see you, they will murder you.'

'Look you but sweet, and I am proof against their enmity.'

He was a boy, laughing and boasting. He was a man. Even from so far away I could feel his warmth. But he could lose his life here.

'I would not for the world they saw you here,' I whispered.

'I have night's cloak to hide me from their sight.' He added softly, 'If you love me, then let them find me here. My life were better ended by their hate, than lived long but wanting of your love.'

'How did you know where I was?' Had he bribed a maid, little Joanette perhaps?

'By love.'

He said it so simply I knew that it was true. He had known where to find me as surely as I had known his face in the banquet hall.

He smiled. 'I am no pilot, yet were you as far as that far shore washed by the farthest sea, I would adventure for such merchandise.'

Suddenly I wondered if he thought me too bold. Guigemar's lady had not done what I had done tonight. A girl should wait for a man to speak first, not call out into the night. Was he adventuring? Would he boast tomorrow that he had won the Capulet girl?

I said quickly, 'Do you love me? I ... I know you'll say you do. And if you say it, I'll believe it. But, gentle Romeo, if you love me, pronounce it faithfully.'

He said nothing, looking up at me. Was he hunting for words that might convince me?

I met his eyes. 'If you think I am too quickly won, I'll frown and be perverse and say thee nay, so you will woo me. But trust me, and I'll prove more true than those who have more cunning to be strange.'

Would he never speak?

I said in a small voice, 'You overheard me speaking of my true love's passion when I didn't know you were there. Pardon me. I did not yield so quickly because my love is light. It was covered by the night.'

A breeze stirred across the garden. It was as though the wind was his fingers. Parts of my body woke in aches and shivers. I felt my breasts against my shift. I had never thought of my breast as different from my chest. I wanted him to touch me. I had never wanted that before. Servants had touched my body all my life. This was different.

At last he seemed to find the words. Each one was low, distinct: 'Lady, by yonder moon I swear —'

'Oh, swear not by the moon, the inconstant moon.'

'What shall I swear by?' His voice was as serious as mine.

'Do not swear at all. Or swear by yourself, and I'll believe you.' I glanced around the shadows of the garden. I should not be here, alone with a young man, and in the night, dressed only in my shift. No matter what love Romeo might swear to me, how could he think me virtuous? I had never spoken with a man alone in all my life, not even with my brother or my father. I had to leave!

I bent over the balcony to whisper again. 'Though I have joy in you, I have no joy in this contract tonight. It is too rash, too unadvised, too sudden. Goodnight! Goodnight! As sweet repose and rest come to your heart as that within my breast.'

He moved forward, so close I wondered if he meant to try to climb the vines up onto the balcony. 'Will you leave me so unsatisfied?'

I stepped back, wary. 'What satisfaction can you have tonight?'

He moved no closer but met my eyes. Dark eyes, like mine. 'The exchange of your love's faithful vow for mine.'

I had misjudged him. Misjudged myself. 'I gave you mine before you did request it.'

'Would you withdraw it?' His face looked as young and uncertain now as mine must have been.

I said softly, 'My bounty is as boundless as the sea, my love as deep. The more I give to thee, the more I have, for both are infinite.'

I heard Nurse mutter in my bedroom: 'Juliet? Poppet?' Then with alarm: 'Where is the girl?'

I had to go. 'I hear some noise within,' I told Romeo. 'Dear love, adieu!'

'My little lambkin?' The bed creaked as Nurse got up.

'Anon, good Nurse!' I called. I gazed down on my love again. 'Oh, strange, to be so near, and yet so far away. Sweet Montague, be true.'

I heard his final words as I pushed back the curtain: 'Oh blessed, blessed night. I am afraid, being in night, all this is but a dream, too flattering sweet to be substantial.'

Was it a dream? I looked at Nurse. No one would ever dream of Nurse. She stared back at me, smelling of wine and brandy.

She burped slightly. 'My poppet, what is it? What's wrong? Is it your stomach? All that rich food?'

'Not my stomach, but my heart. Oh, Nurse, I have lost my heart.'

She stared at me. I heard her silence, loud as the church clock. Twice in my life had Nurse been silent, and both today and yesterday. At last she said, 'I heard a man's voice out in the garden. Not Paris? Nor Tybalt either?'

I shook my head.

Nurse was no fool, though she could sound one. 'That young man tonight, the Montague?'

I whispered, 'His name is Romeo.' I waited for Nurse to call the Joans, the footmen, to alert the house guards to cast him out.

Instead, she said, 'What do you feel, my lambkin?'

'That my heart is twisted into his, and will be for all time, and his with mine.'

'Ah.' For the third time Nurse was silent. Finally she reached over and took my hand. 'I had a heart that loved a man like that. All the world, it seemed, was him and me. A good man, and a kind one.'

I had never heard Nurse talk like this, deep from her heart. Was it the wine that stopped her chatter and made her words true? Or had she glimpsed in me what she had felt once too?

I whispered, 'What happened?'

'The plague,' said Nurse. 'When I was seven months with his child. They locked me in the house with him, in case I had it too. Most in those houses died together, when one man had the plague. I sat with him and I watched him die. I wanted to die at that moment, but

I had the babe inside me to think of, my Susan, his and mine. "Let me out, let me out!" I screamed. But instead they nailed the door shut. "Give me food!" I shouted. "Of your mercy, give me water to drink!" But no one even threw a loaf through the window.

'Forty days they kept me locked in there. I held a pot out the window to catch the rain to drink. I ate dry crusts, and then I ate nothing, for there was nothing left to eat, and all the while his body lying in the room upstairs, his bright young body that I loved, now bright no more. On the fortieth day they let me out. But my Susan was dead inside me, from sorrow and from starving. I cried then. I could not waste water in tears for him before. I cried for him and for my Susan. But then I had you, my poppet.' Nurse suddenly looked fierce. 'And I would give my life and heart for you. So you tell that man out there that if he loves you truly, he will wed you afore he beds you. And if he can't say yea to that, he is no man to love. But if he will, why then you take him, even if he is a Montague.'

I stared at her. This was the one marriage in all the world I could not have. No romantic dreams would serve me now. Nurse could marry where she wished. But I, a Capulet ...

Reality slipped over me like cold water. I had been a moonlit girl. It was time to be a woman. Had Guigemar's lady let herself die in that dungeon? No, she had sought out her love! Who said I could not marry a Montague? Was it the Church, or the Prince? No. The Holy Church liked two lovers wed. As for the Prince ...

My skin prickled. This marriage could be an answer to all his woes.

Who better to marry than a Capulet and a Montague? Our marriage would heal the Prince's city. Romeo's parents and mine would forbid us if they knew. But what could they do once we were married? My father had one child only, as did Lord Montague. They would have to forgive us. The quarrel would be mended, and by my hand.

It was as though I had turned the page in Marie's book, and found it ended happily. A girl would bring two broken families together. A girl hand in hand with her true love, just like in the stories.

I kissed Nurse quickly on her fat cheek. I stepped back through the curtain. The moon shone like a golden plum hanging over the wall. I knew he would still be there.

His face broke into happiness as I looked down. 'My lady?'

'Three words, dear Romeo, and goodnight indeed. If that your love be honourable, your purpose marriage, send me word tomorrow by one that I'll ask to come to you. Where and what time you will perform the rite; and all my fortunes at your foot I'll lay. I'll follow you, my lord, throughout the world.'

Would he agree? A girl did not propose marriage, and such a sudden one. But he had let me come to him, had let me choose if we should kiss or not. I looked at his face and saw my answer.

Nurse called from within. 'Madam!'

Was she regretting sending me out?

'By and by, I come,' I called to her. I looked at Romeo, his hat off in the moonlight. I smiled, and felt him smile with me. 'Tomorrow I will send,' I whispered.

He bowed his knee, but kept his gaze on mine. 'So thrive my soul.'

'A thousand times goodnight!' I slid back inside. I heard him say, 'A thousand times the worse, to want your light!'

Tomorrow ... tomorrow we would be wed. Tomorrow Juliet Capulet would change the world. I floated on weariness and the scent of roses ...

Nurse took my arm. 'You haven't found when your messenger will meet him, girl! Tell him I'll come to him to take a message from him to you. But he must say when, and where.'

Dear Nurse. Kind Nurse. I ran back out. 'Romeo!'

He was still there. 'My dear?'

'At what o'clock tomorrow shall I send to thee?'

He giggled. Guigemar would never giggle. Somehow I fell even more in love. 'We are poor conspirators. By the church steps, at the hour of nine.'

'I will not fail. 'Tis twenty years till then.'

I stared at him, the square solidness of his body, the shine of his dark hair, his moonlit face. It was as though my whole life had been in waiting, just for this.

I said at last, 'I have forgot why I did call you back.'

He smiled. 'Let me stand here till you remember it.'

I shook my head. 'I shall forget,' I said solemnly, 'to have you still stand there, remembering how I love your company.'

'And I'll still stay, to have you still forget, forgetting any other home but this.'

Suddenly I was aware the moon had sunk below the garden wall. ''Tis almost morning. I would have you gone, and yet no further than a wanton's bird —'

'I would I were thy bird,' he said dreamily.

I smiled at the idea of a small Romeo perched upon my shoulder. 'Sweet, so would I.'

The moon shadows had turned to black. The sky would grow grey soon. The watchman would be here. If Romeo would not go, then I must send him away, to keep him safe.

'Goodnight! Goodnight! Parting is such sweet sorrow that I shall say goodnight till it be morrow.'

I forced myself to step away from him and through the curtain. I heard his words, too loud for safety, too sweet to wish unsaid. 'Sleep dwell upon thine eyes, peace in thy breast! Would I were sleep and peace, so sweet to rest.'

# Chapter 10

I lay on my linen pillows, but my mind soared higher than the stars. I thought of Romeo, his words, his look, the heat of his fingers touching mine.

I thought of myself too. What is a girl? Born of her family, fed by her nurse, dressed by her maids, kept from the world by her garden walls. But I had seen another life: the world where a woman crossed the sea to find her love; where a woman's tales were read hundreds of years after her name and home were lost.

I was writing a story now, like Marie de France. But my story was real. Tomorrow I would unite Verona, where even the Prince had failed. Guigemar's lady's name was lost, but Juliet's would be remembered. In a hundred years people would still know my name.

I was more than my family now, more even than Romeo's love.

I was Juliet.

The nightingale sang. At last I slept, and then I slept too long. The sun was above the courtyard wall when I awoke. Nurse was still snoring, and no Joans had come to wake us. They must think us tired from the banquet.

Today I would be married. Had I dreamed it all? My whole life changed with a few words at a banquet, and an hour in the moonlight and roses. Romeo. I let my lips make his name without a sound. Today Juliet Capulet would be no more, and in her place a Montague.

Dreams need no planning. Marriage did. I had to think.

Marriage was made of more than words. Today's ceremony could be undone, our marriage made nothing, until we had shared a bed. I knew nothing of what would happen in the marriage bed, only that it was something important. A marriage wasn't legal till it was done. If we were discovered before we had shared a bed, his father and mine could have our marriage annulled.

Tonight, Romeo must come up here, to my bed. How? Through the halls? Impossible.

I dozed again, and woke as the church bell rang eight. Nurse sat on her truckle bed, staring at me. Her expression was hard to read.

'The Earl of Paris is a fine man,' she said, as if we had been talking for the past hour. 'A flower of a man, the Prince's cousin too. And that song he sang about you —'

'I marry Romeo today.'

She looked uncomfortable. Was she regretting her midnight words in the light of day? Had she drunk too much wine last night?

'Ah well. Romeo,' she said. 'Yes. But are you sure, my dove? I remember your dog, what was its name? You loved it too. Cried and cried you did when that dog died. But the next day, the smiles were on your cheeks again.'

Poor simple Nurse. I was the dagger that would slice away the enmity between the Capulets and the Montagues, more powerful than Tybalt's rapier.

I smiled at her. 'Nurse, darling Nurse. He is my love, and I marry him today. Call the Joans. It is past the breakfast hour.'

Yesterday I had been a child for Nurse to chide. Today I gave the orders. The touch of his lips and his hand on mine had done all that. What would tonight give? I shivered as Nurse pulled the bell.

Nurse left as the bell rang nine, sailing off in her best skirts, winking at me while the Joans dressed me, saying she must go to the market to buy ribbons as I had torn my best last night.

I ate. I sat. I waited. I could not write or read or draw or play my harp. I did not want the company of the Joans. Time dragged like a crust through a bowl of honey.

I waited while the clock struck ten, eleven, noon, and still she did not come. Love's heralds should be thoughts that are ten times faster than the sun's beams, not a fat-legged nurse.

At last I heard her footsteps. I pulled aside the curtain and there she was, Peter the page behind her, holding a package that must contain the ribbon.

'Oh, honey Nurse, what news?' I asked. 'Have you met him?'

Nurse looked at me warningly. 'Peter, stay at the gate,' she said.

I waited till the page had vanished down the corridor, then let the curtain slip back. 'Now, good sweet Nurse.' I tried to read her expression. 'Oh lord, why do you look so sad?'

Had he changed his mind? Had Nurse even met him?

'I am weary,' she said. 'Give me leave awhile. Fie, how my bones ache! What a jaunt I have had!'

'I wish you had my bones, and I had your news! Now come, I pray you, speak. Good, good Nurse, speak!'

'Do you not see that I am out of breath?'

My heart was midnight ice. 'How are you out of breath when you have breath to tell me that you are out of breath? Is your news good or bad?'

'Well, you've made a fool's choice. Romeo! His face is good, and his legs. But he is not the flower of courtesy.' Nurse peered at the table. 'Have you dined yet?'

'I wasn't hungry. What says he of our marriage? What of that?'

'How my head aches. It would break in twenty pieces. Oh, my back too. Here I've been, trudging back and forth for you —'

'Sweet, sweet, sweet Nurse, I am sorry that you are not well. Tell me, what says my love?'

'Your love says, like an honest gentleman, and a courteous, and a kind, and a handsome, and, I warrant, a virtuous ... Where is your mother?'

She was teasing me. She had to be teasing me. Or delaying the bad news. 'My mother is within. Where should she be?'

'Is this the poultice for my aching bones? You can do your messages yourself.'

I sat on the bed, my hands in my lap, an obedient child to her nurse again. 'What says Romeo?'

She smiled. At last she smiled. My heart melted, just a little.

'Have you got leave to go to church today?' she asked.

'I have.'

'Then get you to Friar Laurence's cell. There stays a husband to make you a wife.'

The world spun. The colours faded, then came back too bright.

Nurse looked at me, amused. 'Now comes the wanton blood up in your cheeks. Get you to church. Now I must find a rope ladder, so your love can climb to his bird's nest as soon as it is dark. I am the drudge and toil for your delight.' She grinned at me. 'But you shall bear the burden soon at night.'

My cheeks did flame then.

Nurse bent and kissed me, smelling of sweat and the honey pastry she must have eaten at the market. 'Go. I'm going to find my dinner. Get you to the friar's cell.'

By myself? I looked at her. Nurse might be my secret messenger, but if she were a witness at my marriage my parents would dismiss her, casting her out to starve. Even when I was married to Romeo, perhaps his father might not let Nurse join me. She could only help me so far.

But I didn't need a nurse now. I was Juliet, and I would change the world.

'Hie to high fortune.' I hugged her. When next I saw her, I would be married. 'Honest Nurse,' I whispered, 'farewell.'

# Chapter 11

I called for my chair. It was made of cedar wood, sweet smelling, with damask cushions and curtains in Capulet green. The footmen trudged on either side as we bobbed down the street. I kept the curtains shut. I smelled the sawdust and vomit stink of the tavern, the stench of chamber-pots, the blood smell of the butchers' row.

The smells changed as we reached the marketplace. Someone yelled, 'Oysters, fresh oysters!' The apple seller shouted, 'Codlins ho!' Someone cried, 'Buy sweet lavender!'

Sweet lavender. Sweet Romeo.

It seemed a thousand leagues across the marketplace. We must be by the baker's now, the scent of the morning's hot crusts still in the air. The smell of ale and sweat and stew, the clucking of hens and flap of pigeons as we crossed the square, the clatter of hooves from some noble's horse.

At last Peter drew the chair's curtains at the church steps. He handed me out. I thanked him for the courtesy. I lifted my skirts and climbed the stairs.

'Pretty lady! Pretty lady!' the beggars called as they glimpsed my silks. A man with no arms darted forth, his cap held in his teeth. A hunchback grovelled at his side, and a small boy who had no legs but slid on a small trolley with wheels.

I shook my head at them to show I had no money. They accepted it, seeing I had no maid or footman to carry coins.

I stepped past the woman with scars for a face and the girl with white eyes, and into the dimness of the church. I genuflected and crossed myself, then slipped to the side door and out again, using the damp path above the graveyard. I could smell fresh earth and baking bread from the friars' kitchen.

The friars' cells were built with their backs to the cliff, of the same stone but mossy, each with a bench outside and a small door. Most of the rooms had been empty since long before I was born, when the King had ordered the monasteries disbanded, but a few of the friars had stayed, bound to the new church now, giving lessons and guidance to the young.

Which cell was Friar Laurence's? I should have asked.

One door stood open. Suddenly it seemed that I had done this a hundred times, a thousand. *This* was the door. *This* was what I had to do, had always had to do.

I peered in. The friar smiled at me from the room's shadows. He might have been a shadow himself, middle-aged and thin, in his brown robe and sandals.

I tried to find my voice. 'Good even to my ghostly confessor.'

'Romeo shall thank you, daughter, for us both.'

The friar stood aside, and there was Romeo. He looked the same. He looked quite different. This was no moonlit smile now, but a husband come to claim me. If I were older than I had been last night, then so was he.

'If you are as happy as I,' he said quietly, 'then it seems impossible that this should make us happier.'

I smiled at him, both bold and shy. 'My love is grown to such excess, I cannot sum up half my wealth.'

He took my hand and bent to kiss me. His lips were warm. There was nothing in the world but him and me ...

Friar Laurence cleared his throat. 'Come, come with me, and we will make short work! You two shan't stay alone till holy church make two in one.'

We parted, guilty, but my hand stayed clutched in his. I felt half-terror and half-joy.

Back along the path we went, into the church again, quiet at this hour save for a nun praying to one side. She stood as we came in.

I kneeled with Romeo. The friar stood above us and began to pray.

'Dearly beloved friends, we are gathered together in the sight of God ...'

But there were no friends gathered here, no family, just Friar Laurence and the sister standing as witness by our side.

A bride should remember all her marriage words. I remembered little. Just Romeo's closeness and his smile; the beams of sunlight drifting through the windows; the fear that someone might interrupt before the friar was done. But no one spoke.

'Wilt thou have this woman to thy wedded wife, to live together after God's ordinance in the holy estate of matrimony? Wilt thou love her, comfort her, honour and keep her, in sickness and in health? And forsaking all other, keep thee only to her, so long as ye both shall live?'

Romeo met my eyes. Our glance held. He was telling me that although this was all so fast, his vow was true.

He said, 'I will.'

Friar Laurence looked at me. 'Wilt thou have this man to thy wedded husband, to live together after God's ordinance in the holy estate of matrimony? Wilt thou obey him and serve him, love, honour and keep him, in sickness and in health? And forsaking all other, keep thee only to him, so long as ye both shall live?'

I did not pause. 'I will.'

'Who gives this woman to be married unto this man?'

My skin prickled. My father was not here to give me away! But Friar Laurence took my hand, then Romeo's, and bound us two together.

'And now please say after me ...'

Romeo repeated the words, each one quiet and clear, his gaze still on mine. 'I, Romeo Montague, take thee, Juliet Capulet, to my wedded wife, to have and to hold from this day forward, for better, for worse, for richer, for poorer, in sickness and in health, to love and to cherish, till death us do part, according to God's holy ordinance, and thereto I plight you my troth.'

He let go of my hand. For a moment I felt bereft, till Friar Laurence gestured to me that I should take Romeo's hand in mine again.

I said the words steadily. I knew them from my cousins' weddings. And what girl has not said them under her breath, imagining when they would be her own?

'I, Juliet Catherine Therese Capulet, take thee, Romeo Montague, to my wedded husband, to have and to hold, from this day forward, for better, for worse, for richer, for poorer, in sickness and in health, to love, cherish and to obey, till death us do part, according to God's holy ordinance, and thereto I plight you my troth.'

Romeo reached into the pocket of his doublet and drew out a ring. It gleamed in the church's shadows, gold, with a circlet of rubies. It was too large to be a woman's ring. Perhaps it had been a present from his godfather or his grandfather. Now it was mine. He slipped it on the fourth finger of my left hand. I had to clench my fingers a little to keep it on.

'With this ring I thee wed, with my body I thee worship ...'

I flushed at the thought of the night to come.

Romeo smiled at me, but his voice was steady. '... and with all my worldly goods I thee endow: in the name of the Father, and of the Son, and of the Holy Ghost. Amen.'

We prayed, the friar's voice over us.

At last we stood. The friar said, 'I pronounce that they be man and wife together. In the name of the Father, and of the Son, and of the Holy Ghost. Amen.'

More words. So many words. I heard them not, not any one of them. For we were wed, his hand in mine.

Finally we kneeled again, to receive Communion, then walked, still hand in hand, to the room behind the altar. I had never been there before, had not even known that it existed, but only had eyes for my new lord.

We signed a book, and then some papers. I used my old name for the last time: Juliet Capulet.

I walked from that room as Juliet Montague.

# Chapter 12

The friar gave us a half-hour together in his cell after the ringing of the bell. No more, or my family might wonder why I tarried so long at church.

We sat on the narrow bed in the cell while Friar Laurence sat on the bench outside. For a moment I was afraid my new husband might want to consummate our marriage then and there. My body wanted him, but not like this, in daylight, with the friar at the door. Besides, I had no idea what I was supposed to do. If this had been a proper marriage — and yet it was, I told myself, for all its haste and secrecy — my mother might have prepared me.

I glanced at Romeo. Did I imagine it, or was he as nervous as I was? He took my hand and kissed it; no lingering lover's kiss, but one a knight might give his lady. He kept my hand in his.

'Well,' he said.

'Well,' I said at almost the same time.

And suddenly we were giggling as though we were five years old, not husband and wife, not lovers who had defied their families, nor the couple who would yet unite them and bring peace within the city's walls.

'I think,' he said, his voice tentative, 'that night's love must wait till night.'

I nodded.

'You're not scared?' he asked.

'Of … of night matters? No,' I said, although I was.

'Of what our families will say tomorrow?'

'Tomorrow and tomorrow and tomorrow,' I said. 'The Prince will be our friend.'

He stared. I saw he had not thought about our union in this light. It struck me deeper than a dagger, that he had risked his name and fortune, all for me.

'The Prince will have his wish,' I said softly. 'Our houses are united. You will be the heir to the House of Capulet.' I met his eyes. 'My lord husband, a Montague, will guide it as my father has.'

He looked at me in wonderment, then kissed my hand again. 'I will.' It was a vow as solemn as those we had made in church. 'And you will be the empress of my heart, and chief gentlewoman of our land.'

We smiled at each other in the dimness of the cell. I could see our future rolling out before us, like a footman rolls out a carpet, the years, the days, the hours, spent with my Romeo. Our grandchildren on our knees, our robes of heavy silk. The combined house of Montague and Capulet would be the greatest trading house in all of Europe. I saw us receiving guests at a banquet, the Prince bowing over my hand, and Lord Paris too, not my lord at all but just another guest. I would be gracious.

We were married. It was done. There would be anger from our parents tomorrow, but not for long, not once the Prince gave us his blessing. Nurse must send Peter with a message to the palace … No, I now had a husband who should do that.

As if he heard my thoughts, Romeo said, 'I will go directly to the palace and ask a private audience of the Prince.'

'Pray him not to tell our fathers,' I said. 'We must have this night together first, so they can't undo the marriage. Then we will tell our fathers what we have done.'

'When the clock strikes ten tomorrow,' he said, 'we tell the world. Let the church bells ring again, for Juliet and Romeo are wed.'

For the third time he lifted my hand to his lips.

The friar cleared his throat outside. 'My Lady Montague,' he said, and I started as I realised that now that was me. 'Your men will wonder where you are.'

We stood. My husband kissed me then. I had thought a kiss a brief dry thing. This was long. I tasted him. He tasted of himself, a scent so sure and strong. The kiss went on and on, growing deeper, closer …

'My Lady Montague.'

I broke away, but still our gazes locked. I wished we had not spent the half-hour talking, but had kissed instead.

My husband whispered in my ear, 'Tonight there shall be a new bright star, made from our love today. Its light will guide all lovers along love's bright flowered way.'

I had no words to say to him, no artful phrases. I smiled, and let the friar lead me from the cell, while my husband waited behind so that none would see us together.

Yet.

# Chapter 13

I sat on the cushions on the balcony, but I did not sew. I sent the Joans away. I watched the petals on the roses in the garden below. I looked at the garden wall. Beyond it was my love.

I wished that fiery horses would drag the sun down the sky; wished to close the curtains on the day. Let Romeo fly here on the wings of night. I had bought the mansion of my love, but not yet crossed the threshold ...

Tonight he would come and claim me, with the Prince's blessing. Tomorrow, my mother would glare, my father shout, but I would be gone, my hand in my husband's.

I tried to imagine the days after that. We would breakfast in our rooms at first so I would not have to face Lord Montague, for he would be angry too. But surely his anger would pass as he realised his son would now inherit the Capulet wealth?

I tried to imagine the next Christmas feast, with our families at the table together, a babe in my arms with eyes like Romeo's. But I could see nothing. How could I dream my love so clearly and not be able to see our years ahead? Why could I imagine Guigemar's long life, happy with his love, but not my own?

I knew before Nurse told me. Knew the moment I heard her step. A shadow struck me, cold as night.

Nurse pushed the curtain aside. Her hands held the rope ladder that would bring my husband to my room. She threw it down as though it were made of snakes, her face shadowed like a mid-winter cliff. I ran into the room.

'What news?' I asked. 'Nurse, tell me fast, what news!'

'He's dead. He's dead! Lady, we are undone. He's gone, he's killed. He's dead!'

'No!' I would have felt his death, a knife ripping us apart. 'Not Romeo.'

Nurse sat on my bed and wailed. 'Oh Romeo, Romeo. Whoever would have thought it? Romeo!'

I grasped her shoulders. 'What are you, that you torment me thus? Has Romeo slain himself?'

Nurse covered her face with her big hands. 'I saw the wound, saw it with mine eyes. Pale, pale as ashes, all bedaubed with blood. I swooned at the sight.'

I whispered, 'Oh, break, my heart! Poor bankrupt, break at once! Let the earth take me, so I and Romeo share one bier.'

Nurse rocked her body back and forth. 'Oh Tybalt,

Tybalt, the best friend I had! Oh courteous Tybalt, that ever I should live to see you dead!'

'Tybalt?' I said. 'Is Romeo slaughtered and Tybalt dead too? My dear cousin and my dearer lord? Who is living if those two are gone?'

'Tybalt is gone,' Nurse wept, 'and Romeo banished. Romeo that killed him, he is banished.'

The earth shifted once again. 'Oh God! Did Romeo's hand shed Tybalt's blood?'

'It did. It did! Alack the day, it did!'

Two hours ago Romeo and I had been hand in hand, and wed. Two hours, and his hand had killed my cousin. Who had I married? A serpent heart hid within a flowering face? A vile book bound in a sweet cover? A few hours ago I had been a warrior wielding a sword stronger than any knight's to bring peace to Verona. Now I was a girl, lost in the world of hate and men.

'There's no trust, no faith, no honesty in men. All are perjured, all forsworn, all naught, all dissemblers,' Nurse wailed. She reached under her pillow for the flask of whisky I wasn't supposed to know she kept there. She pulled out the stopper and took a swig. 'These sorrows make me old. Shame to Romeo!'

Romeo. The world steadied.

I knew the man I had married. Romeo loved me. He had never breathed an insult to my name of Capulet. I was a beast to think that Romeo could do wrong.

'Blistered be thy tongue!' I told Nurse. 'He was not born to shame: no shame would ever sit upon his brow.'

Nurse looked at me, amazed, the flask in her hand. 'Will you speak well of him that killed your cousin?'

'Shall I speak ill of him who is my husband? You think him a villain, to kill my cousin? My cousin was a villain, to try to kill my husband.'

For a moment the breeze blew clean again. I wiped away the tears I had not realised I had shed. Then I remembered. Romeo was banished. I had lost everything. My husband, my future, the hope of our two houses mended together. But most of all, I had lost my Romeo.

I tried to find my voice. 'Where are my mother and father?'

'Weeping and wailing over Tybalt's corpse. Will you go to them?'

'Have they called for me?'

Nurse shook her head.

'If they haven't called, they do not need me. My loyalty is to my husband, not to them. They can wash Tybalt's corpse with their tears.'

An icy sea swept through my heart. What could I do now? I had been married, but wasn't yet a wife. I still did not know what men and women did in the marriage bed, but I did know that if we did not do it tonight, our marriage could be annulled.

I would have to marry Paris ... I couldn't, even if I had wanted to. I was another's now.

The world was grey. My sun had gone. I was lost in a dark tunnel.

I picked up the rope ladder from the floor. 'Poor ropes,' I whispered, 'you are beguiled, both you and I, for Romeo is exiled. He made you for a highway to my bed. But I, a maid, die maiden widowed. Come, ropes; come, Nurse. I'll to my wedding bed, and death, not Romeo, shall take my maidenhead.'

Nurse stared at me, her mouth open. 'I'll find your Romeo. I know where he is.' She sounded panicked at my despair.

Her words were a light in the dark. 'What say you?'

She sighed. 'He's hid in Friar Laurence's cell. I'll bring him to comfort you.'

I blinked at her. One night together, I thought. One night instead of all our lives. But in that night I would truly be his wife. It was a small gift when so much was lost.

I pulled off the ring Romeo had given me. 'Give him this, to show that it's no Capulet trick.'

Nurse looked at me grimly. 'I'll bid him come to take his last farewell.'

I sat in my room, but left the curtains open. I looked at the sky, so blue that it seemed impossible tears of rain could ever cloud it. I would die rather than marry the Earl of Paris and betray my love. I did not want to die, but Juliet Montague could not go back to being Juliet Capulet, the obedient girl who would marry the man, or boy, her father chose for her.

Did dying hurt? Living hurt, so I supposed dying did as well. I wanted so much to live.

And I was alive. I had a whole night before me, with my love. Tomorrow I would think of a world with no Romeo in it. Tomorrow, I would think of dying.

If this would be the only night of love I had, I would cram a lifetime into every hour.

I stood up slowly and pulled the bell.

# Chapter 14

The Joans arrived, their smiles gone. Little Joanette looked as though she had been weeping. Had she loved Tybalt, that smiling fool who had killed my future?

I would not think of Tybalt now.

I said abruptly, 'I have been crying too much.' Let them think it was for Tybalt. 'I wish a bath, then bed.'

'My lady,' began Janette, 'we are so sorry about your cousin.'

'Not now,' I said.

Joan and Janette carried in the bath, a china one from a far land, with peacocks painted on it. Peacocks, like poor Tybalt. They brought jugs of warm water, scented with lavender. Lavender eased sorrow. Today its scent was not enough.

Be happy, I told myself, as I let them soap me, dry me, powder me, slip a linen shift over my head. You must be happy.

I felt neither sorrow nor anger. So much life and death and love, all in a single day.

The Joans left, taking the bath, leaving the fire built up with logs of apple wood and dried lavender to scent the room. I sat before the flames in my linen shift and dried my hair, then pulled a comb through it. It caught in the tangles. I had never combed my hair myself before. I used my fingers to undo the knots as best I could, then combed my hair again. It sat in a cloud around my shoulders.

Outside, the shadows lengthened. The cries of the far-off market quietened. And still Nurse did not come with Romeo.

Had he left Verona already? Was Nurse eating dinner in the kitchen to avoid facing me with the news? Or had she gone to tell my mother?

No. Nurse was loyal.

I should feel something. Anger. Pain. Eagerness for my husband. But it was as though I was locked in a room of ice that the fire could not melt.

At last I heard Nurse's step along the corridor, slower than I'd ever heard it before. I tried to feel the excitement I had felt this morning, but that was gone too.

I looked up from my cushions. 'Well?'

'He is coming. Like the soot from a fire, you can depend he'll come.' Nurse sat heavily on a cushion and looked at me. 'He'll be a monkey, climbing the garden wall as soon as it's dark.' She nodded at the rope ladder

I'd half-hidden under my bed. 'But he'll need the ropes to get to you. Oh, I'm that tired. My bones ache worse than in winter, and my feet, galloping here and there ...'

I lifted the ladder, interrupting her complaints. 'From where should I hang it?'

'You twist it around the railing ... Oh there, I'll do it.' She heaved herself up, took the rope ladder from me and wound the top part around the balcony, twisting it to make it secure.

I went back and sat by the fire. Nurse sat across from me, her eyes closing. The flames crackled and spat. The scent of lavender filled the room. Her mouth opened for the first snore. I said, 'Nurse?'

'What?' She opened her eyes again. 'What is it, my pigeon wing?' She sounded more weary than I had ever heard her.

'What ...' I stumbled over the words. 'What must a bride do on her wedding night?'

Nurse opened her eyes properly at that. 'Why, her husband's will, that's what.'

'But what is that?'

'Bless the child, there's no need for you to worry over it. Thy Romeo will know it all. Although, of course, the groom is young. But young or not, he is a man.'

One night, I thought. Only one night. I have to do it right.

'But what do *I* do?' I asked.

101

My anguish must have reached her for she patted my hand. 'You lie there on the bed, that is all. The groom will do the rest.'

'Just lie there?'

'And shut your eyes is best, so you don't see what's coming and be afraid.'

'But ... but why should I be afraid?'

'No reason in the world,' said Nurse airily. The thought of marriage beds had perked her up. 'The pain is less than nothing. And besides, it don't last for long, not if your groom's eager, as your Romeo will be. Oh, my Simon, never was there a better man. In and out he was each time, before I'd time to blink. It's what happens out of the marriage bed that counts, so you just think of that, though with your Romeo banished it's not a thing to think on.'

I stared at her. Emptiness grew around me.

Nurse reached for her whisky flask, under her pillow. 'Such a fine husband, my Simon was. He'd have me eat my fill before he ate his when I was carrying our Susan and the bread price rose. He put the best of the salt beef on my plate, not his. A jewel of a man he was, and we were so happy until the plague took him. Ah, a plague on all the plagues.'

'Then tonight ...' I began.

'Worry not about tonight, my poppet.'

She did not say, 'You have made your bed, now you must lie in it.'

The watchman had just called 'All is well' when I heard a scratching below the balcony.

Nurse pushed herself to her feet again. 'Well, he is here, or else it is a squirrel, but didn't I see them put the squirrel traps out myself, so it must be him. I'll call the girls to bring a pallet to the corridor. If anyone comes, I'll tell them you're tired with weeping, and have set me as a guard so you may be alone. And true enough, I've been a guard to you ever since I held you in my arms ...' Her words ran out. She stared at me.

'Thank you,' I said. I could not tell what she was feeling. I did not know what I felt myself.

'I'll be on watch, my sweeting. I'll be in earshot if you call.' She left.

I should have gone to the balcony to greet my husband. I didn't. I stayed by the fire.

'My lady? Juliet?' He stood there in the dark, the firelight on his face.

'My lord.' I tried to smile.

He didn't kiss me. He didn't touch me. He sat on a cushion on the opposite side of the fireplace and watched the flames. His face looked thinner, his eyes darker. I made no move to touch him.

At last he said, 'It was an accident.'

'Do you speak the truth?'

He looked at me, then, 'No. Tybalt killed my friend, Mercutio. Stabbed him like a dog, all for a joke. I stabbed your cousin then so my friend's soul would not ascend to heaven by itself. I killed Tybalt in anger, with no thought of you. And that is the truth.'

And I had asked for it. 'Do men ever think of women when they fight?'

'I do. I mean ... I will. I ... I've had no practice as a husband.'

'But much at sword play.'

'No more than any other man. Nay, less. I tried to stop them fighting. Tried to curb your cousin's anger, told him even that I loved the name of Capulet. I was on my way to see the Prince as I had promised. An arrow plucked from the air just by mischance, that hit us both.'

I said nothing. He could have walked on. Walked away. Left Tybalt to the Prince's anger.

'Juliet, my love, give me your face, your smile. Mercutio's men saw the fight. They will tell the Prince that Tybalt struck first, that I hung back till Tybalt killed Mercutio. Friar Laurence says we must have patience, not despair. Mercutio was the Prince's cousin; he is grieving for him too. The Prince will forgive me.'

His words melted the prison of ice that had stopped me thinking or feeling since I had heard the news. Spring began to flower through the snow. 'The friar truly thinks the Prince will let you return to Verona?'

'I must stay away long enough for your family to bury your cousin. All summer, at the least.' He took my hand. I did not draw it back. 'Our winter shall be warm,' he whispered. 'We must think of that, when summer aches with drought of love.'

'Where will you go?'

'My family has land near Mantua, far enough to quench your family's anger. Near enough so I will still drink the same breeze as you.'

'Then take me with you!'

'If I could, I would. My love, I must ride hard tomorrow, before your family's revenge bites.'

He was right. Of course he was right. He was a man, and I a girl. When I rode, it was balanced side saddle, not as a man rides. I had never galloped, never even ridden for long. When we travelled to our estates, I was carried in my chair. I would need men to carry me to Mantua, to keep me safe. Romeo would be in more danger if I were with him, forcing him to travel slowly.

'I will write to the Prince,' my husband said softly. 'I'll ask for his forgiveness, as I beg for yours now. If you will let me be your husband truly tonight, then we are wed, and I can tell the Prince that the war between our houses ceases from this day.'

So there was hope. No, not hope. Certainty. Spring's green shoots became a rose. It was not long till winter. Winter, and my Romeo.

I managed a smile. 'Well, husband?'

'Well, my wife?' And then he asked gently, 'Are you scared?'

'No. Yes. A little.' I wanted to ask, Do you know what to do? But, unlike me, Romeo had not lived his whole life behind a garden wall. 'Yes, I am scared,' I said.

One night, I thought. And then: I must keep each heartbeat, every breath. This is my summer, to keep me till the leaves turn gold in autumn, till snow lays a path for my returning husband.

Lie back, Nurse had said, and with the Earl of Paris I might have done just that; let my husband take my body, his by law. But not with Romeo. I had walked to meet him: at the banquet, and on the balcony, and then to church to marry him. I wanted to *do* now, not simply be. But do what?

His finger stroked my neck, a kiss of butterfly wings. And suddenly my body knew it needed him. His skin upon my skin. His breath mixed with mine.

For a second I held back, hoping he thought me beautiful, with my short body, my dark hair. He met my gaze. I realised he was as uncertain as I was.

But he was all wonder, the warmth of him, the solidness, the joy growing in his eyes as he looked at me. I had not known my love for him could grow, but it did then, as I knew he wanted me to find beauty in him too.

He pushed the shift from my shoulders so it puddled at my feet. My hands were at the buttons of his shirt, helping him to pull it off. Man and wife are one flesh, said the marriage ceremony. This was the magic of the night. My flesh yearned for his, skin on skin and breath on breath, so close that we were one.

I pressed my body to his. I let my hands explore him, every shape and shadow. His hands found me.

My body was heat and darkness.

This was the night. And it was ours.

# Chapter 15

The nightingale sang in the pomegranate tree outside the window. Romeo's skin glowed silver in the moonlight as he sat up beside me in the bed. He touched my hair, then kissed my lips again, swollen from the night.

'Did you like that?' he whispered.

I kissed him instead of answering. We had been clumsy that first time, wanting to explore the secret places but uncertain what was allowed in the dance. Our bodies and our hands knew each other the second time, knew each other's love, and pleasure. And after that I did not count ...

'I think it must get better with practice,' I said.

He smiled. 'We will practise a lot. Practise for every icicle of winter, warm each other in each gale. Juliet will be my sun, even under snow clouds.'

I stroked his shoulder: hard muscle and soft skin. So this was what Guigemar and his lady had done. They had not just sat together reading in the garden. This was why the Queen had survived in that dark dungeon, had crossed the wild sea. She had survived for this.

'With my body I thee worship,' I whispered.

I felt the strength of him, ran my fingertips along the short hairs on his arms, then the muscles of his stomach. The body that had looked a little dumpy stuffed into layers of clothing was compact and strong now. Why did men cover themselves in silk and velvet when there was so much beauty underneath?

The nightingale sang again, long and sweet. Romeo bent his head and kissed me again, a long soft kiss, not like the bruising kisses we had exchanged as the hours tolled across the night. He swung his feet to the floor.

'No!' I clutched his hand. 'That was the nightingale, not the morning lark.'

'It was the lark.' He spoke softly. All night we had been quiet, a small nation made of two. 'Night's candles are burnt out. I must be gone and live, or stay and die.'

'That isn't the dawn. It's a meteor to light your way to Mantua. Dear love, stay a little longer. You need not go yet.'

He looked at me seriously. 'I'll stay, if that is what you wish. I'll say the grey is not the dawn. I'll say the lark is but the nightingale. I want to stay more than I want to go. I'll say to death "welcome" if Juliet wills it so. See, it is not day ...'

I could not bear to hear him speak of death. 'It is daylight! Be gone, away! It is the lark that sings so out of tune. More light and light it grows.'

He whispered, 'More light and light, and more dark and dark our woes.'

'Madam.' It was Nurse's voice, urgent, outside. 'Your mother is coming to your chamber.'

'Quickly!' I said, but still I could not let him go.

He took my fingers gently from his arms and kissed them, then kissed me on the lips again. He shrugged into his shirt and hose, grabbed his shoes and stockings. I pulled my shift back over my head, and ran out onto the balcony after him.

'Art thou gone? My lord, my love, my friend. I must hear from you every hour, for in a minute there are many days.'

'I will. Farewell. One kiss and I'll descend.'

His lips touched mine for three heartbeats, then he climbed swiftly down the ladder. I watched him run between the rose beds, then climb the pomegranate tree against the garden wall. For a moment he stood among its branches, looking back at me, a shadow against the dawn, his face as white as Tybalt's in his tomb.

No, I would not think of death, nor sorrow. We would meet again, and soon. Now I was a wife — his wife. Nothing could stop me now.

I looked at the tree again, as though his shadow might have left a mark. But he was gone.

'Juliet?'

I turned. 'Mother?'

My body was still moist with him, my lips bruised. Surely she would see?

My mother's dress was black, her coif too. Even her slippers were black satin. Her beads were jet, and glittered as the first sunbeams flickered across the garden and onto the balcony. Was she up early? Perhaps she hadn't been to bed, but had sat with Tybalt's corpse through the night.

'I ... I am not well,' I said.

'Still weeping for your cousin's death?' How could she not notice the signs of love? Did she ever really look at me, except to see the duty of a daughter? Her face was colder than stone. 'Tears will not wash Tybalt from his grave. Too much weeping shows lack of wit, not grief. Better you weep because the villain lives who slaughtered him.'

'What villain?'

'That same villain, Romeo.'

I stepped into the bedroom. My body still smelled of Romeo, of us. I hoped that the scent of roses and lavender would cover it.

'God pardon him,' I said. 'I do, with all my heart.'

She looked at me incredulously. I had to be careful. She would expect me to be angry too. How many weeks or months must I stay here and pretend?

I said cautiously, 'I wish that mine would be the only hands to take our vengeance.'

My mother smiled. 'We will have vengeance, fear you not. I'll send to one in Mantua, where that banished runagate shall live. I'll send him such an unaccustomed dram that he shall soon keep Tybalt company in the earth. And then I hope you will be satisfied.'

Poison! My heart clenched so hard it hurt. My mother's still room held many medicines that could kill in the wrong dose. The sword was a man's weapon. Was poison a woman's? Last night I had learned what my mother had never taught me about love. What had she not taught me about death?

I had to get a message to Romeo. Perhaps through Friar Laurence ...

I said automatically, 'Indeed, I never shall be satisfied with Romeo till I behold him ...' That was true enough. I added, 'Dead ...' I stopped, hearing my words. They belonged to a good daughter, not a good wife. I should not say them, not even to stop suspicion. I said carefully, trying to find words that would still be true to Romeo, yet not alert my mother, 'If you could but find a man to bear such a poison, I would temper it, that Romeo should soon sleep in quiet.' And let it be, I prayed. Oh, let him be safe in sleep tonight.

I looked at my mother. I doubted she had even heard my words.

'Now I'll tell thee joyful tidings, girl,' she said.

'Joy comes well in such a needful time,' I responded. A nice girl's words. Obedient. I must play their game till winter. 'What are they, madam?'

'Well, you have a careful father, child. One who will sort your sorrow with a day of joy.'

'What day?'

'Early Thursday morning, the gallant, young and noble gentleman, the Lord Paris, at St Peter's Church, shall happily make you a joyful bride.'

A marriage in two days' time! How? Why? It was as if the nightingale had become a vulture. 'No!' I said.

She stared at me. She had not thought I even knew such a word.

Somehow my voice swept on. 'I will not marry yet! And, when I do, I swear, it shall be Romeo.'

My mother's eyes grew as hard as her black beads. I wished I could gulp the words back.

I added quickly, 'Who you know I hate, rather than Paris.'

Boots clapped on marble in the corridor. My mother looked at me grimly. 'Here is your father. Tell him so yourself and see how he takes the news from you.'

My father entered, Nurse at his heels. He was dressed in black too, black that sucked in every other colour in the room. He looked more tired than grieved. His daughter was just another duty to get done in a long hard day. My mother loved Tybalt, I thought, but all you have suffered is an insult to our house.

'Still crying, daughter? Your tears will make a flood, your sighs a wind.' He looked at my mother. 'Well, wife, have you told her?'

'Yes. But she will none, and gives you thanks. I wish the fool was dead.'

I had always known she would have gladly exchanged my brother's death for mine. I bored her. Disappointed her. But this?

My father rubbed his eyes. 'She should be on her knees, to thank us, proud that so worthy a man will be her bridegroom.'

'I ... I can't be proud,' I said. 'I hate the thought of marriage after all that has happened.' Tybalt had caused my grief. Let him be the excuse to keep me from marrying Paris now. 'I thank you, indeed I do, but —'

'"Proud"? And "I thank you"?' My father stared at me as if I were Tybalt's poor wolfhound got to its hind legs to argue with him. Weariness swept into fury. 'Thank me no thankings, nor proud me no prouds, but get your fine legs ready on Thursday, to go with Paris to St Peter's Church, or I'll drag you there on a stretcher.'

I wished I could be stone, like the statues in the hall. A statue had no father or mother, that her heart should freeze like this. What was a daughter? Nothing, when she refused to be what her parents wanted her to be.

'Father, please.'

'You baggage! You tallow face!'

His yells hit the marble walls. I heard their echo down the corridor.

I kneeled in my shift on the floor. It was as though I pleaded for a million daughters. Pleaded to be myself, not just a daughter, a possession like his ships. 'Good father, I beseech you on my knees ...' I had never asked him for anything. Not his love, nor even his notice. 'Hear me with patience but to speak a word!'

'Hang thee, young baggage. Disobedient wretch! Get thee to church on Thursday or never after look me in the face. Say nothing, don't reply, don't answer me. My fingers itch.'

He lifted up his hand to slap me. I cowered back.

'Wife, we scarce thought ourselves blessed to have but this only child! Now I see this one is one too much.'

He grasped me by the hair. I screamed. His hand slapped my face, once and then again.

'My lord ... you are to blame, my lord, to scold her so.' It was Nurse. My dear Nurse.

My father stared at her. 'Hold your tongue!'

'I speak no treason, sir!'

'You mumbling fool! Speak with the other gossips. I want none of it here.'

His face was red. His hands shook as they gripped my hair. I bit my lip to stop crying with the pain.

My mother murmured, 'Sir, you are too hot-tempered.'

My father dropped me, so suddenly my elbow cracked against the floor. 'Hot?' he repeated. 'God's bread, it makes me mad! Day, night, hour, time, work, play, all my life has been to have her matched well, a gentleman of noble parentage, stuffed with honourable parts, and then to have a wretched snivelling fool to answer, "I'll not wed. I cannot love. I am too young. I pray you, pardon me."'

He stared down at me, as if I were a beggar in the street. 'Thursday is near, and you are mine,' he added coldly. 'I'll give you to my friend. If you refuse, you can beg in the streets, hang, starve, die, for all I care. I won't acknowledge you. For what is mine shall never do you good. Trust to that, my girl. You have my word.'

He pushed past Nurse. She curtseyed, trembling, remaining with her head bent low till he was gone.

I lay where he had shoved me, on the floor. I looked up at my mother, her eyes as black shadowed as her dress. 'Is there no pity sitting in the clouds? Oh, sweet my mother, cast me not away! Delay this marriage for a month, a week. Or, if you do not, make the marriage bed in that dim monument where Tybalt lies.'

My mother was silent. I thought she listened to me. But when she spoke it was with more contempt than I had ever heard.

'Do as you want, for I have done with thee.' I heard the silk of her dress sweep across the floor and out the door.

# Chapter 16

I sat on the cold floor in my shift. My hair was down and knotted, my feet bare. No wonder my parents had not listened to me.

No, it made no difference what I wore or what I said. I was theirs, to do with as they wanted. All I'd ever known was what they had given me: life, the silks I wore, the pearls, the dancing master. But none of it for love. If they loved me, they would have listened to me. My parents had created their daughter as my father would have shipwrights build a ship: for its use and the wealth it would bring him.

But I was not a ship. I was Juliet. And I owed my parents nothing now.

I said in a small voice, 'Nurse? Have you any word to comfort me?'

She sighed. 'Well, here it is. Romeo is banished, and likely he'll not come back. So perhaps it is for the best that you marry Paris.'

I stared at her.

She went on more quickly. 'Oh, Paris is a lovely gentleman. Romeo's a dishcloth to him. I think you're lucky in this second match, for it exceeds your first. Your first is dead, or as good as. A husband gone away is no use to you, nor you to him.'

'You speak from your heart?' I asked her.

'And from my soul too.'

Nurse's hands had tended me all my life. I thought she loved me. Loved me like her Susan, whom she had tried to save through the forty days of plague, caring not for her own life, but her child's.

But I was not her Susan. Nurse cared for me. But she cared more for herself, her comfortable life. I had been alone for all my life and never known it. My mother, my father, had not known me. Even Nurse had abandoned me.

There was only one who loved me. Somehow, some way, I had to get to Romeo in Mantua. Even the anger of the Montagues, which I would surely find there, could be no worse than what my family had done.

I closed my eyes. I prayed. And when I opened them, I knew what I must do. Friar Laurence would know where Romeo was. The good friar might even help me.

I turned to traitor Nurse. I said abruptly, 'Well, you have comforted me marvellously much. Go and tell my mother that I'm going to Friar Laurence's cell to make confession for having displeased my father.'

Would Nurse believe it?

Her face cleared. 'I will, and this is wisely done!'

As if my heart would change as fast as hers. 'Ring for the maids. And for fruit. I wish for fruit.'

'Of course, my locket. Ah, your appetite is back at last. There's preserved quinces in the kitchen, I saw them myself, and cherries, and an apple pie —'

'Fresh fruit,' I said. 'Oranges or a pomegranate.'

'But fresh fruit is indigestible on an empty stomach —'

'Oranges,' I insisted, and turned my back on her.

She left. I waited for the Joans to come to dress me and bring the oranges. With them would come a knife, a long sharp knife to cut the fruit.

If I could not get to Mantua, I would need a knife.

# Chapter 17

I would not let them wash me. Let them think it was grief for Tybalt's death. I wanted my husband's scent to stay with me, to know it was there under my clothes.

Joan brought me a black petticoat, black overdress and grey sleeves. At first I thought it was to suit my mood, but then remembered our house was in mourning for Tybalt. I had never seen the clothes before. Perhaps they were my mother's; or kept for just such a case as this and quickly altered during the night to make them fashionable. The hat had a loose veil to hide my eyes, my nose, red from so much crying.

None of the Joans spoke. Nor did Nurse — it was the longest time I had known her to go without saying a word. At last they were finished. Nurse picked up her cloak to come with me.

I shook my head. 'I will go alone.'

'But, my little dove —'

'I'll go alone.'

Nurse had given me a night with Romeo just as she had tempted me with honey cake when I was small, to stop me crying. Our love for each other was no honey cake, to give and then take back. Her heart was with her Susan, not with me. I had been a plaything, to fill the place Susan had left.

I pulled down my veil. Little Joanette darted to open the door curtains. As she held them back, she whispered, 'I'm sorry about your cousin.'

'Joanette!' hissed Joan. A serving maid did not speak unless her mistress spoke to her first.

'It's no matter. Thank you, Joanette.' I hesitated, then pulled a black ribbon from the trimming on my sleeve. 'Wear this, with my thanks.'

Joanette curtseyed. 'Yes, my lady. Thank you, my lady.'

A good child. I tried to imagine a future where I might take her into my own household, mine and Romeo's. I held my love like a small warm ball against my heart. It was all I had to anchor me in the shattered tumble of what had been my home.

I had to get to Mantua.

My chair jogged and swayed above the cobblestones. The knife was cold inside my sleeve. Once I had planned to be the knife that would sever our families from their hate. Now I was being blown like a small leaf on the winds of fate.

Romeo. His name was a talisman to keep me steady. I could still smell him, faintly. No, not his scent, the scent of us together.

My head ached with grief. My mind was dazed. My body longed for him.

I felt slightly sick, but also as if my body floated somewhere else. I had not slept last night, nor much of the night before. I pinched myself hard, to try to think. There was no time for dozing now.

How to get to Mantua? I had no money. Even if I had, what was I to do with it? Who would hire a horse to a girl? A few great families kept carriages, but there were none for hire. When I had travelled before, it was only to our own estates for a brief time in the summer or when the plague raged in the city. The litter curtains were always drawn, for modesty. While they prevented the common folk seeing me, they also prevented me seeing where we were going, except when I peeped out between the curtains. Could I hire chairmen to carry me to the city gate, and to keep going till they came to Mantua?

But travellers needed food. They needed inns with rooms prepared for them, the fires lit, the sheets aired, the beds warmed, the hot water waiting. The household steward did all that. I realised I did not even know how much it cost to buy a loaf of bread.

I should have asked Romeo to hire men from Mantua to bring me to him! Stupid, stupid girl.

But if I had not stayed, I would not have discovered the threat of poison that still might strike him down. I tried to think which poison my mother would use. Foxgloves? Two drops could help the dropsy. Four could kill. Bitter almonds? One crushed into a hundred sweet almonds gave almond paste a rich flavour, but death followed hard and painfully if it were eaten alone. Even the hemlock my mother dropped into her eyes to make them sparkle in the candlelight could kill if given to a man to drink. Well, she had taught me a cure for her poisons too — a paste of rue and figs and walnuts. Friar Laurence must send Romeo the recipe. He must eat some of the paste each time he took food or drink.

My thoughts drifted to Mantua ... was it a city just like ours? Faraway places had dragons, monkeys, elephants. Did Mantua have those?

I lay back on the cushions and shut my eyes, then opened them in case I wasted time in sleep. Think! Once I was gone to Mantua, my father would disown me. He would not break a vow. Would the Montagues disown their son too, for marrying a Capulet? Were Montagues kinder parents than Capulets? If both families disowned us, how would we live? Jewels were worth money, I thought vaguely. We could sell my jewels. My father would disown me, but he probably would not abandon my children.

I almost smiled. Children; mine and Romeo's. Blood of my father, and of his father too. No matter what the son and daughter did, their children would be innocent, and the only blood relatives our fathers had. Blood called to blood.

If the Prince was happy with our marriage, he might decree that we be called back by Christmas-tide, allowed to live under his protection. Perhaps the Prince too had wept last night, for his cousin, slain Mercutio.

The chair stopped. Peter drew the curtains and helped me down. I climbed the stairs, not even glancing at the beggars, then hurried through the church and down the path.

The friar's door opened. A man came out. For a moment my heart stopped, thinking it was Romeo. He had not yet left for Mantua. We could go together!

It was the Earl of Paris. He wore pink stockings, puffed-up gold breeches and a wide hat with three long feathers. It made him look younger, not older as perhaps he'd hoped.

He swept the hat off and bowed. 'Happily met, my lady and my wife!'

My skirts were too wide to get past him on the narrow path. I tried to keep my voice calm. 'That may be, sir, when I may be a wife.'

He smiled. 'That must be, love, on Thursday next.'

Fear clutched at my heart. I kept my voice steady. 'What must be shall be.'

Friar Laurence stepped out from the shadows of his cell. 'That's a certain text,' he said grimly.

The Earl grinned. It was a good grin, not like his courtly smiles. 'Come you to make confession to this father?'

He was different, here in the open air. Gentler; no prancing dog showing off his new bone. Perhaps he had been pretending at the banquet, just as I had been, each in the role expected of us. But I was not his wife yet, nor ever would be.

'To answer that I should confess to you,' I said.

The Earl laughed. 'Do not deny to him that you love me.'

I felt my cheeks flush under my veil. Did he think that my father could promise him my heart as well as my body?

'I will confess to you that I love him,' I countered.

'So will ye, I am sure, that you love me.'

He looked happy, as if I were his already, meek and obedient, the perfect wife. And so I should have been, perhaps, if the last two days and nights had never been. He'd have had the shell that was the proper daughter, well trained to be a proper wife.

I could bear his face no longer. I looked at the ground. 'Love being spoke behind your back will be of more value than to your face.'

The Earl reached out and lifted up my veil. I wondered what my face must look like: blotchy with tears, red and swollen from my father's slaps. Whatever he saw in it was not what he expected. The laughter faded and he touched my arm gently.

'Poor soul, thy face is much abused with tears.'

There was true kindness in his tone now. Kinder than either my father or my mother had been. Perhaps the shell of Juliet could have been happy with this boy. Perhaps even the girl inside too. It did not matter. I belonged to another now, in heart, in body and in law.

I tried to pull away. 'My face was bad enough before the tears.'

'Your face is mine, and you hast slandered it.' His voice was soft.

Was it a compliment to me, or to himself? Had I been wrong, that night at the banquet? Did Paris love Juliet, and not her father's wealth? But my heart was my husband's, and my body too.

I said briefly, 'It may be so. My face is not mine own.' I looked to Friar Laurence. 'Are you at leisure now, holy father?'

'I am free.' He stepped from his cell, solid in his cassock.

How much had he seen and known in his long life, this old man who had lived through the wrenching away of one faith, and lived now with another? Who had heard the confessions of so many souls year after year?

'My lord, we must entreat the time alone,' he told the Earl.

The Earl bowed, to the friar, not to me. 'God shield that I should disturb devotion. Juliet, on Thursday early I shall rouse you. Till then, adieu, and keep this holy kiss.'

His lips were on mine before I could stop him. He tasted of wine and ginger this time, sweeter than before. He stepped back and bowed again, this time to me.

I wanted to spit his taste out on the path. Not because it was foul, but because it was not Romeo's. My lips belonged to my husband and I must keep the memory of his kisses.

Instead, I curtseyed, then pulled my veil down again as the Earl stepped past me. He was whistling as he strolled back to the church.

It was dim and cool inside the cell, and smelled of the spice scent that came from long years of prayer. It smelled of earth and moss too. I shivered.

'Please, shut the door,' I said.

The friar looked at me, his face hard to read. 'Lord Paris won't be back, my daughter.' But he shut the door.

'Come weep with me,' I whispered. 'Past hope, past cure, past help.'

The friar's eyes were uneasy. He would break God's law if he married me to Paris. If he did not, he faced death or exile.

'I already know thy grief,' he said. 'You will be married to Lord Paris on Thursday. Nothing I said would make him delay the wedding.'

'Tell me not of weddings unless thou tell me how to prevent it.'

He shook his head. He looked even older, his face sagging and wrinkled. So, I thought, you do not have the nerve to tell the Capulets you have married their daughter in secret to their enemy. If you do not have the courage, then it must be mine.

I took a breath, and drew the silver knife out of my sleeve. It felt warm from my body. Who listened to a girl? No one, not her mother nor her father. The good friar too would dismiss my words.

But he could not dismiss a knife. Killing myself would be a sin, a sin to prevent another sin, marrying another when in the sight of God I was my husband's. Would the death and damnation of a girl give the friar pluck enough to help me to my husband?

I held the knife out to him. My hands did not even tremble. 'God joined my heart and Romeo's; thou our hands. And ere this hand, by thee to Romeo sealed, shall be the label to another deed, this bloody knife shall be the umpire. If you have no remedy, then I will die.'

The friar stared at the knife, then at my face, as if I were new to him.

'You mean it,' he whispered.

I said nothing. I did not know if I could kill myself. Would not even try to answer that until all chance of living with my Romeo was done. I heard the drip of water from the rock face and the faint cries of the beggars by the church.

The friar ran his hand through his thin ring of hair. I've made you think, I thought. At last he spoke. 'Hold, daughter. I do spy a kind of hope.'

'What? Tell me!'

'It's as desperate as that which we would prevent. If, rather than marry Paris, thou hast the strength of will to slay thyself — well, if you dare to do this thing, I'll give thee remedy.'

My heart beat hard against my chemise. 'Oh, bid me leap from the battlements of yonder tower than marry Paris, or bid me lurk where serpents are.' I gazed at him, desperate to convince him. 'Chain me with roaring bears, or shut me at night inside a tomb, covered with dead men's rattling bones, or bid me go into a new-made grave, and hide me with a dead man in his shroud. I will do it without fear or doubt, to live an unstained wife to my sweet love.'

The friar bit his lip. 'Hold then; go home, be merry, give consent to marry Paris —'

'But —'

He lifted his hand for silence. 'Tomorrow night, before the wedding, look that thou lie alone. Let not thy nurse lie with thee in thy chamber.'

He kneeled and pulled a box from under his narrow bed, then opened it. It was filled with dried herbs, of the kind friars used to help the poor when they were sick, and small stone jars filled with medicines. He picked up a vial and looked at my face.

'Drink this when you are in bed. Your veins will run cold. Your pulse will stop. No warmth, no breath, shall testify that you live. The roses in your cheeks and lips shall fade. You shall be cold and stiff and stark, like death.'

Even a good friar has poisons, I thought. How much have I never seen from my room above the garden?

The friar waited a moment, perhaps to see if I would scream, or faint. I did not. He nodded, almost to himself.

'You shall continue in this state for two and forty hours,' he said, 'then wake as if from a pleasant sleep.'

I shook my head, dazed, weak from hunger and lack of sleep. How could this help me get to Mantua?

The friar continued. 'When your bridegroom comes to wake you in the morning, there you are, dead.'

I thought of the graves outside; of lying in the cold ground in my coffin, of waking to the company of bones and corpses. The friar saw my thoughts on my face.

'No,' he said quickly. 'You shall be borne to that ancient vault where all the Capulet kindred lie, dressed in your best clothes, laid on top of your bier. I shall send letters to Romeo. He and I will sit by your bier till you awake, and that very night shall Romeo bear thee hence to Mantua.'

I couldn't think clearly. No one would expect Romeo to come back so soon. No one would see us in the darkness of the graveyard. The friar's plan seemed as far from real life as a story from one of Marie's tales. But it might work. And it was all that he could give me.

The friar looked at me steadily. 'And this shall free thee of thy present shame, if no inconstant toy nor womanish fear abate thy valour in acting on it.'

I was not ashamed! The friar was the one who had sinned, thinking I might marry another while my husband lived. Womanish fear? I was the girl who would unite the city and end a centuries-long feud.

I met the friar's eyes. 'Give me! Tell me not of fear.'

He handed me the vial. It fitted my hand as if it had been made for it. Its glass was cold, despite the warmth of the friar's hand.

'Get you gone,' he said quietly. 'I'll send a friar with speed to Mantua, with letters to your lord.'

'Tell him my mother plans to have him poisoned,' I said. 'Warn him to take care!'

The friar did not look surprised that my mother planned to kill a Montague.

'Romeo will be here before she can harm him,' he said. 'Warn him yourself.'

'Love give me strength,' I whispered. I pushed the vial up my sleeve, next to the knife.

# Chapter 18

The curtained chair bounced along the streets through the crowd.

Even my bones felt tired, as if each were made of stone. Would the friar's plan work? It had to work! My tired mind could find no other way. To die, and then to wake. To wake in my Romeo's arms. Two days, and I would see Romeo again. Two days!

I shut my eyes. I could not bear to play the good daughter, the betrothed wife of Paris, for two days. I would take the poison tonight. And if Romeo and the friar were not there when I woke up, then it would be better to lie in the darkness of the tomb, the bones of my kin around me, than in the house of my parents.

Tybalt's body would be there too. I shivered, and opened my eyes.

Poor Tybalt. Poor angry boy. I had not liked him, but I had loved him, just a little. He had been part of my life. Now, at last, I truly realised he was gone. All that he might have been was gone as well. Perhaps if he had become head of our house, he might have steadied once he was sure of his position, lost his anger. Now all was gone: the good, the bad, the might have been. Suddenly the tears for Tybalt came as well. Romeo and I had hope and lives to come, each other's arms and laughter. Tybalt had nothing but his tomb.

Better a day and night with Tybalt's dead body in that tomb, with the smell of death and darkness, better even rats, than to pretend in my father's house for one more day.

Now I knew that I would escape, I could get through this afternoon, and this night too. A few hours and Juliet Catherine Therese Capulet would be gone, and Juliet Montague waiting for her love.

I checked that the vial and knife were safely up my sleeve, then prepared a face and speech to greet my father.

My father was in the hall with my mother and Nurse, the steward and a cluster of our servants. He gave me a hard sharp look, then gestured for the servants to be gone. I forced myself to smile. His angry look softened.

'How now, my headstrong! Where have you been gadding?' he asked me.

I curtseyed. 'Where I have learned me to repent the sin of disobedient opposition to you and your requests.' No nice girl could have said it better. I rose from the curtsey, then stepped closer to him and kneeled at his feet. 'I am enjoined by holy Laurence to fall prostrate here and beg your pardon. Pardon, I beseech you! Henceforth I am ever ruled by you.'

My knees were cold. I looked at my father's velvet shoes. Black, with jet embroidery.

I felt my father's hand on mine. 'Stand up!' His face had turned to sunlight.

Fool, I thought. Were all old people fools?

He clapped his hands for a footman. 'Send for Paris,' he ordered. 'Tell him of this. I'll have this knot knit up tomorrow morning.'

Tomorrow or the day after, it didn't matter to me now when Paris thought the wedding would be. Either way, I would be gone.

I said carefully, 'I met the youthful Paris at Laurence's cell and gave him what love I might, not stepping over the bounds of modesty.'

My father looked as if his world was as neatly embroidered as a tapestry again, each person in their place and his daughter nothing but a shadow of his wishes. 'This is as it should be! We owe this friar our thanks.'

One day, I thought, you shall know exactly what thanks the friar deserves.

I turned to Nurse. 'Nurse, will you come and help me dress for tomorrow?'

For the first time my mother looked disturbed. 'No, not till Thursday! There is time enough.'

Poor mother. Stupid mother. Worrying about a wedding banquet to prepare by tomorrow, a daughter and herself to dress.

My father shook his head. He would not risk me flying my cage now. 'We'll go to church tomorrow.'

I wished I could tell my mother that there was no need to rush about preparing a banquet tonight. I wished … I was not sure quite what I wished. For a moment I felt my lover's hand upon my skin, his fingers running through my hair.

Would my parents mourn me when they found what looked like my dead body tomorrow morning? No. They would not mourn the inside me; only the loss of the daughter who would have joined their house with the nobility. A loss more like the sinking of a Capulet ship than the death of a cherished child. You'd mourn the loss of a ship, but that did not mean that you had loved it.

My father waved me away. 'Nurse, go with her.'

I heard him discussing the wedding decorations with my mother as we left.

My room had never seemed a prison before. Silk bed curtains, velvet cushions, tapestries on the walls, the scent of roses from the garden. No rats, no darkness, like the dungeon of Guigemar's lady. I had not even realised I had been as trapped as she.

Nurse bustled in behind me. 'I will send the girl for thy dress, my lambkin … Oh, it is such a dress!'

'Bring me a mirror,' I told her.

She stared. 'You may look at yourself in your mother's once the dress is on.'

'Bring me one. Now!'

Nurse gestured to the Joans. A short time later, I heard the footmen on the stairs, carrying a mirror up from the hall. They propped it against a wall.

I nodded to the Joans and to Nurse. 'Go. Good Nurse, please leave me to myself.'

'My poppet …' She looked at me for a moment, then left the room.

I knew she would not go far. She would be listening at the door, peering around perhaps. It did not matter.

I looked at myself in the mirror. No, not at myself. At the black taffeta dress, the underskirt, the bodice, the ruff, the hair in its gold snood.

Slowly, silently, I slipped off the snood, the overdress, the petticoat. The ruff and sleeves took longer. I had not realised there were so many pins.

At last I stood there in my shift. I let it crumple onto the floor.

Now there was only me. Just Juliet. White skin. Dark eyes. The breasts that his hands had stroked. My rounded knees. This was what he had seen. His wife. Now I had seen it too.

No one else in this world, except for Nurse and the Joans, had seen me like this. But servants didn't count.

I was Juliet and I was his. I stood there and I vowed that all this was his alone, and always would be. No other man than him.

I lifted the shift from the floor, put it on, and moved towards the bed. I think I cried. I do not know. I knew nothing, except that the day lacked him.

Then I called for Nurse, and for the Joans, and for my wedding dress.

# Chapter 19

The underdress was silver, the overdress cloth of gold, trimmed with pearls along the sleeves and cuffs and in long braids all down the overskirt. Only the wife of a man of royal blood could wear cloth like this. So my parents had always hoped for a noble marriage. Poor Tybalt, hooked with empty hopes.

The dress was too big. My parents must have hoped I would grow to be tall like my mother. The Joans pinned and tucked it; yawning, for the hour was late. But I must be dressed now, to be ready in the morning. There was no time to get the dress right today and then spend another two hours unpicking it, just to dress me again tomorrow in time for church. More stitches, more pins. The candles flickered down to stumps. Little Joanette brought fresh ones.

'Are you hungry, my lady?' she asked.

I shook my head. I was light-headed from lack of food, but wanted nothing that might blunt the poison's bite.

Then I realised that Joanette had asked because she was hungry too. It had been a long time since our last meal. If I did not eat, the Joans would get no proper dinner either.

'I could eat a little,' I said.

'Ah, she's excited, aren't you, my pet? Fine as the sun you are in that bright dress, and a fair groom waiting for you tomorrow. And, oh, the house you'll have. Glass in every window. Even the Earl's privy has a window, so they say, with glass in it, and forcing houses for pineapples, and big pots of oranges too. Oh, you'll even eat asparagus and apricots in mid-winter, and jewels on every finger ...'

Nurse babbled faster than usual, as though words could fill up the emptiness between us. We had lost each other somewhere this afternoon. We both knew it, though neither of us spoke of it.

Joanette left and returned carrying a tray covered with a linen cloth, Peter at her heels with two big jugs of ale.

'Such a fuss in the kitchens!' she panted. 'No one will sleep at all tonight! The boys are turning a whole ox roasting on the spit for your wedding feast, and chickens and pheasants. The footmen are still bringing more from the farms, with torchlight to see their way! The hall is filled with jellies cooling and blancmanges and a hundred great big pies.'

'A hundred sucket spoons I have to shine,' said Peter. 'And a hundred forks. Every bit of Venice glass in the house to be polished, and your lady mother has sent out to borrow more china plates.'

'The bakehouse will be glowing all the night,' added Joanette. 'There's five hundred jumbles going down there to be baked. Then they'll be gilded —'

Nurse glanced at my face. 'Hush, girl. Put the tray down and get back to your pins.'

Joanette set out the dishes on the table. Loaves of golden saffron bread; sweet cubes of jellied milk dotted with gold leaf; mutton in lemon and sultana sauce, all golden too; all from the wedding feast. Gold is the feast's theme, I thought. Capulet gold married to Paris's blue blood.

I ate a cube of jelly, then nodded to the Joans to eat their fill. They didn't stop their work to eat, but wiped their fingers on a linen cloth between each bite.

They finished at last. The Joans cleared away the pins, the ribbons, the sewing baskets. Little Joanette lifted up the tray with its smears of food. She lingered at the door.

'You wish to speak, Joanette?'

'I ... I have been happy in your service, my lady. When you are in your new house ...' She bit her lip.

I said gently, 'When I have my own household, I shall ask my mother if you may share it, as my own first maid.'

'Oh, my lady!' Joanette flushed with pleasure.

She bobbed a curtsey, making the tray tilt, then quickly straightened it before the dishes fell. I heard her singing as she hurried down the corridor.

'Listen to her!' said Nurse. 'Singing like a dairy maid! And a girl that young to be your maid!'

I gazed at the woman of gold and pearls in the mirror. Only the half-ruff was white, to frame my face and bosom. They had even dusted my hair with gold, and netted it with pearls. More pearls hung in three great ropes around my waist, then down my skirt.

I thought: I am beautiful. But any tavern wench would have been beautiful dressed like this, even with dark shadows under her eyes, like mine. And the pearls are worth money, and the dress too, if my Romeo has need of it.

'There,' said Nurse, as proudly as if I were her own Susan. 'Now you lie down and I'll put cushions round you. It will never do to have this gown crease. Fine as the sun it is. I'll sit up and make sure you don't roll in your sleep —'

'No.'

She stared at me.

'I pray thee, leave me to myself tonight. I … I need to pray.'

Nurse knew well enough what I should be praying for. If I were truly marrying the Earl of Paris tomorrow, the marriage would be a sin, for I was already married in the sight of God to Romeo. So many sins …

The door curtains parted. My mother stood there. She was also dressed for the wedding, in green silk and taffeta slashed with red and rubies. She examined me, then smiled. Her maids had whitened her teeth too.

'Do you need my help?' she asked.

'No, madam. So please you, let me now be left alone, and let Nurse this night sit up with you. For I am sure you have your hands full in all this so sudden business.'

My mother nodded. I had no doubt she had a hundred uses for another pair of hands. I was dressed and settled, and there was no need for her to think of me till tomorrow.

'Goodnight,' she said, and looked at my white face, my shadowed eyes. 'Get thee to bed and rest, for you need it.'

My mother and Nurse left with no other word. I watched them go. I had thought that perhaps my mother might kiss me on the last night of what she thought was my maidenhood, but it seemed she did not want to muss my dress, or hers.

Farewell, I thought. God knows when we shall meet again.

I reached under my pillow. My fingers found Romeo's ring, now on a gold chain. I hung it around my neck, hidden beneath my ruff and dress. I reached under the pillow again for the vial of poison and, last of all, the knife.

I had never felt so alone.

# Chapter 20

My body was beyond sleep. Soon, perhaps, I would sleep too long. I looked at the small vial. A poison that would keep me sleeping till my Romeo could come for me. It had seemed the only way when Friar Laurence spoke of it in the shadows of his cell. But now, as the last of the sunlight slipped away from my garden, the friar's plan seemed as fantastic as a play.

There was another way, a better way. I must go to Mantua, tonight.

If Romeo were found when he came to fetch me from the tomb, he would be put to death, either by my kin or by the Prince. Even if he weren't discovered, he would still have the task of spiriting me away.

I was the girl who had dared to ask her love to marry her! Surely it could not be so difficult to get myself to Mantua? People went there every day and then came back.

Thank you, Master Scholar, I thought. At least I knew where Mantua was. Our estates were to the south and

Mantua was also south of Verona. All I had to do was find the road to our estates and then keep going.

My thoughts felt as if they were swimming through jelly. Guigemar's lady had found a boat conveniently to hand. I had no boat, but a chair could be hired. I had seen the chair bearers waiting for clients after church. They must be paid, though, and I had never handled money. I had never seen my mother with money either; our footmen handed over the coins for any hat or ribbon she chose.

How many coins did it take to hire a chair to go to Mantua?

I had no money. But Nurse had her savings, from her wages. Romeo would pay them back. Perhaps she would not even miss the coins till they were repaid.

I reached under the mattress of Nurse's truckle bed. Yes, there was the silk purse, with coins inside. Enough to get me to Mantua? To pay for food and lodging along the way? If it were not, my Romeo would pay the chair bearers what else I owed. And once we got to Mantua, everyone would know the Montague estate if I asked for directions to it.

The friar's messenger to Romeo would go by horseback, far faster than I could travel in a chair. But once we were on the road, I would keep the chair curtains open. I would see and hear Romeo galloping towards us, call out to him to stop. Perhaps he would know I was near without my calling, just as he had found my garden two nights ago.

There was one problem only. The farthest I had ever walked alone was from my chair into the friar's cell. But I was Juliet Catherine Therese Capulet Montague. I would stride across the world.

I leaned over and looked under my bed. The rope ladder lay coiled like a sleeping snake.

I lay stiff in the gold cloth of my wedding dress and waited for darkness. A draught blew through my room, warm and smelling of roast pig. Slowly the house quietened, apart from faint voices from the kitchens. The servants there would work all night on my wedding feast. I wondered if they would be allowed to eat the banquet food when they found that I had gone, or if the leftovers would be given to the poor. Perhaps my father, in his fury, would order the foods burned in the furnace.

My body screamed for sleep, my mind for peace. But there could be no rest yet.

I stood, careful of my wedding dress, then realised I had no need to be gentle with it. I could not travel to Mantua in a dress made of cloth of gold. Nor could I climb down a ladder in a farthingale. I moved to the door curtains, my stiff skirts rustling, and peered down the corridor. It was empty.

I crept down the corridor to the closet where Nurse hung my clothes and furs and linen, lifting my skirts so they did not rustle against the floor. I had never been in the closet before, though I had glanced inside at the dresses, petticoats, sleeves and cloaks all hung around the hole where the chamber-pots were emptied. The smell kept away the moths. The holes were cleared at mid-summer, when we left the city for the fresh air of our estates, returning only when the steward said the stench had gone. It would be mid-summer soon, but the room smelled only of roses, dried lavender, orange peel and cloves.

I hesitated. I had never dressed nor undressed myself; nor could a lady's dress be put on without at least one helper to do the sewing and pinning. But I would not meet my husband's people looking less than a lady. I must be dressed in clothes that reflected my rank in society.

At last I chose a petticoat of red silk to go over my chemise, and an overdress of blue, red sleeves, a camisole and a black cloak to cover it all. No farthingale, for no matter how hard I tried I could not bundle one up to carry it. And finally, the silk slippers with a leather sole that I wore on visits to our estates.

I carried the clothes back to my room and dumped them on my bed. I began to unpin my wedding dress. By the time the church clock chimed the hour, I had only one sleeve removed. It would be morning before my untrained hands could do the work of three Joans.

I took my knife and ripped the seams from shoulder to armpit, and then the dress itself right down one side. It did not cut easily, but it was done.

I stepped out of the cloth of gold. I slipped on the petticoat and camisole. I managed to attach them with three pins — they would have to be enough till I could get a maid to help me. The stockings would not stay up so I put them in a bundle in Nurse's purse, along with the ropes of pearls. No one would see my legs under my skirt and cloak.

I looked at the knife, the poison. I had no need of them now. I slipped them back, under my pillow.

I fumbled as I tied the cloak strings. I had never even tied my own cloak strings. How could I possibly find my way to Mantua?

I bit my lip. My body had lived here in this garden, or in the grounds of our country estates, but my mind and heart had roamed the world. I could do this!

I fixed the ladder, as Nurse had done, winding it around the railing and letting it fall. I tried to climb over the railing after it, but my skirts got in the way. I tied them up about my waist as I had seen farm girls do, as I had done myself when I was small and played with my brother.

Over the railing. I grabbed the ladder and somehow found a footing as it swung. I managed one step down. The ladder swayed again and I grabbed the railing to steady myself. Escape was not easy.

But the ground was nearer now. I jumped. I landed hard.

No time to think of bruises. I slipped through the rose bushes, my feet silent on the path, to the pomegranate tree by the wall. I grabbed the first branch and swung myself up, as I had done when I was small. My body remembered how to climb a tree, at least.

I looked down on the wall. I hadn't known that it was topped with broken glass embedded in the mortar. Anyone who tried to climb over this wall would find their flesh slashed as if by rapiers. But Romeo had climbed this wall. How had he done it?

Think, I told myself. What would protect flesh from broken glass?

Padding. Romeo must have wrapped his cloak into a cushion over the shards of glass. A bundled-up petticoat would do as well. I slid down the tree again, wadded my petticoat into a small hard ball, then carried it back up. I leaned awkwardly over to the wall and thrust the bundle onto it. I stepped carefully from the branch onto the cushioned wall. I could feel the glass under my feet, but it did not cut through my shoes; or if it did, I did not feel the pain.

Nice girls did not jump from walls. It had been nearly eight years since I had played with my brother in the banquet hall. My body remembered. Remembered jumping as a little girl. Remembered last night when I had loved as a woman.

It turned out my body had forgotten about landing. I hit the ground roughly, rolling in what I hoped was only mud. My arms ached. My ankle muttered in pain. I ignored them and looked at my cloak. It was too dark to see much, but I could feel the slime. I tried to brush it off, but whatever it was — it smelled worse than slime — did not want to be brushed away.

I turned my cloak inside out, as Nurse had done once when I spilled pomegranate juice on it at the market. (My mother had not let me go to the market again after I spilled the juice and patted a donkey with fleas.) I could still smell the muck even with the cloak turned, but surely there would be an inn along the road to Mantua, with a maid who could clean it.

I was free. It was so strange and so sudden that I felt giddy. No footmen. No Nurse. No father, nor even a husband. I could head for the forests where dragons lurked. Could walk to the harbour and sail away like Guigemar's lady. Here, now, in this dark lane, I was not Juliet Capulet, nor Juliet Montague. I was simply ... Juliet.

Who loved her husband.

# Chapter 21

I reached up to the wall to pull down the bundle that was my petticoat. It was stuck fast. I left it there. I began to walk, limping slightly, keeping close to the wall; not just to find my way, but also because horses left their droppings in the middle of the road, and chamber-pots were emptied in the middle too. The edge of the street near to the wall would be cleaner. I hoped.

And then the wall ended. The solid Capulet wall that had sheltered me all my life. The next wall was rougher; undressed stone instead of stone plastered and painted fresh each season. I felt my way carefully, my fingers to its edges. Surely I must be near the square now, where there would be chairs to hire. Even at night there must be gentlefolk who needed to hire chairs, those who did not have their own chair and footmen?

I was at a corner. In daylight, the road seemed small, but tonight it was vast. I had to turn right, I remembered that, go past the tavern, and the stall that sold cooked apples, where the beggar boy with no hands sat.

Light flickered from the tavern doorway. I heard laughter, but not the kind I heard on Sundays on the way to church. These were men laughing, with words I did not understand, and then a woman's high-pitched giggle. The giggle sounded wrong, not like the genuine laughter of before.

Please, I prayed, let no one see me as I pass the tavern. Please, let there be a chair.

And suddenly there was. The two bearers came at a steady trot up to the inn door, carrying a single upright chair, not a four-man litter like the one my family used. In the light from the tavern door I could see the curtains looked like leather, not brocade, nor was there a house insignia embroidered on them.

The bearers held the chair steady as the curtains parted. A man got out, balding and stout, already drunk, his doublet half-undone. He flicked the lead chairman a coin, then staggered into the tavern. Someone began to sing inside, and the chairmen turned to go.

'Please,' I said. My voice was a child's. These men would not obey a child and carry her to Mantua. I tried to sound like my mother when she noticed I had soiled my hems out in the garden. 'I wish you to take me to Mantua. Now, if you please.'

The chairmen stopped. The man in front lowered his pole, and his companion followed suit. They looked at me.

The first man grinned in the yellow light from the tavern. 'To Mantua? All the way from here?'

'I will pay you well.'

His grin changed. 'You have the coin to go to Mantua?'

'Of course.' I had my mother's tone exactly now. I stepped towards the chair and waited for the men to lift it up, then hand me into it.

Instead, the man just stared at me. 'Let's see the coin first then.'

I lifted Nurse's purse from my belt. 'Here it is —'

My voice ripped as the purse was wrenched from me. One man grabbed my arms and suddenly my back was in the mud, my skirts over my face. I tried to kick. I screamed. I screamed again, wriggling so my skirts fell aside and I could see.

'Help me! Please!'

My words were smothered as a grimy hand covered my mouth. I tried to bite, but he held me too fast. The first man was still grinning. He untied his hose as the other held me down, his stinking body sitting on me, his filthy hands at my mouth.

Why did no one come to help me? Hadn't the people in the inn heard me cry out? Perhaps they heard pleas for help most nights. Had the poor man who had lost his head cried for help before the Montagues sliced it off?

Footsteps ran towards me. A voice called out, 'That you, Gripper?' It was a woman's voice, rough, a woman of the streets, maybe even the tavern wench whose laughter I had heard that Sunday.

'You go back to your business, woman.'

'What happens outside this tavern is my business. You leave her alone. She's just a girl.'

Gripper grinned, showing two yellow teeth. 'A rich one.'

'An' you got her gold. Be off with you or I'll tell Big Margie. You'll get cold tongue instead o' hot pie if she hears o' this.'

Suddenly the filthy hands were gone. The weight lifted off me too. I heard the men's feet tramp away, carrying the chair that could take me to Mantua, the coins in Nurse's purse, the pearls.

I pushed myself to my feet. I would walk to Mantua. I would eat roots and leaves, and drink from the streams. I looked at my rescuer. Her dress was mud-coloured, and so was she. She could have been my age, or forty.

'Thank you. Oh, thank you,' I told her.

She grinned. I saw she had three teeth to Gripper's two. 'Oh, you ain't got no need to thank me yet, duckie. Off with that skirt. And those sleeves.'

'I ... I don't understand.'

'Saved you from rape, didn't I? And the pox, which lasts longer. I know them men. I reckon you owes me more than your pretty clothes.'

'And if I don't give them to you?'

I could run from her. I was young, strong. She looked half-starved.

'Then I give you this.' A knife glinted in the flicker of the tavern's lamps. 'I'll cut your face first, will I? Pretty thing like you. No man's goin' to want you to wife with a scarred face. And I'll cut off a finger, then a slice across your breast.'

My fingers fumbled at my skirt, pulled off my sleeves. The wind bit cold, carrying with it stink and hopelessness. I hesitated at my last petticoat and my camisole.

'All,' she said. Her voice was rock.

'Please ...' It was all I had, a plea to a tavern drab.

The woman-girl hesitated. She slipped off her ragged cloak. 'Fair trade, eh? You get your life and this. I get your silks.'

I clasped her dirty cloak and turned my back, my hands trembling. I slipped the cloak over me, covering my nakedness as the last petticoat fell to the dirt. The cloak covered my breasts as I undid the ribbons of my camisole. It hid his ring, my Romeo's ring.

No hope of reaching Mantua now. But I still had his ring. And I had Friar Laurence's plan.

I would live. And we would be together.

*\*\**

My hands shook. My body felt like it had been ripped by icy claws. I stopped, and shut my eyes till I saw Romeo's face within the darkness. I would not cry. I could not go on if I began to cry.

I opened my eyes and felt for the garden wall. A foothold, and another ... Slowly I hauled myself up onto the cushion of my petticoat. If the glass ripped my flesh, I did not feel it. The wind mocked my nakedness. Only last night, its touch had been warm, the fingers of love. The wind did not care. Even the friar would not stand and admit he had married us. The roses were showy skeletons below me in the garden. The stench of muck covered their sweetness. No one was true. Except my love — our love. It was the one thing pure in the whole world.

My trembling fingers found a tree branch. I had to force them to hold on. Had to force my body to move. My foot reached for a lower branch and missed. My body slid. The cloak tore, and so did my flesh. But all I felt was cold, not pain. And then the ground, hard against my hip and shoulder. I lay there. I could not even breathe.

At the other end of the garden a voice shouted, 'Who goes there?' Darkness moved within the darkness. A house guard.

I found a breath and called, ''Tis I, Juliet.'

I thought the guard would come closer; see my nakedness, the muck, my hair. But he knew my voice; thought, perhaps, I was wandering among the roses, dreaming of tomorrow's wedding.

'Goodnight, my lady.' He hesitated, then added, 'And all joy for your wedding tomorrow. Your lord father is giving every man a golden guinea and a keg of ale to drink your health.'

What use were wedding wishes to me now? But joy — yes, I could accept that wish. Tears stung my cheeks, or was it blood?

I said softly, 'Remember me in your prayers.'

'Yes, my lady.' The guard sounded puzzled that a girl should be thinking of prayer before her wedding. Perhaps he heard the exhaustion in my voice.

I let out my breath as his shadow travelled across the gravel to the next courtyard.

I glanced at the balcony. Was the ladder still there? Had Nurse looked in on me, and seen it, and drawn it up? Was she even now confessing all to my mother?

No. The ladder hung there, limp and waiting. I crawled till I could reach a branch, to help me to my feet. At last I stood upright, the stinking cloak around me. I walked, step after step.

It took me a year to climb. Ten years. My bones were milk jelly. After an eternity I leaned over the railing and half-fell onto the balcony.

I let the stinking cloak drop to the floor. I looked at it, then slowly bent and picked it up. I staggered to the privy hole and threw it down.

I washed in the ewer. I washed and washed to try to remove the stink from my skin, my hair. I dared not call for more water. At last I washed with rosewater, even my hair. Finally the stink was gone.

I was too tired to wait for my hair to dry. Let it dry while I slept. My fingers shook. I looked at them: scratched, the nails broken. They were not mine. No wonder they did not obey me.

I managed to pull up the golden wedding skirt, to pin it onto the shreds of chemise. I slipped my arms into the ripped sleeves without bothering to pin them. What would Nurse and the Joans think when they saw the ripped dress, my torn fingers, the bruises and scratches upon my body? Would they think I had stripped off my wedding dress, then flung myself around the room?

I didn't care. My body could do no more. My only hope was poison.

Nurse and the Joans would dress me to lie in state in death. They would arrange my hair. They would do it all. When I woke in my love's arms, his cloak would keep me warm, and his love too.

Sleep. All I had to do now was sleep. But this would be no sleep. This would be death, until I woke.

I lifted the vial. Its opening stared at me, a single evil eye. What if the poison didn't work? Would I be married tomorrow morning?

No! The knife lay on the table next to my bed. Its blade gleamed in the candlelight. I touched its tip with a clumsy finger and watched a drop of blood fall. I had doubted I could kill myself in Friar Laurence's cell. I had no doubts now. Better the knife than a double sin: bigamy and betrayal of my love.

I uncorked the vial. It smelled of moss, of bones and secret tombs and wolf lairs. What if Friar Laurence had truly given me poison? Perhaps he wanted me dead, to save himself?

No. The friar was a good man. Strong enough to marry us, even if not strong enough to admit it. I trusted him. Perhaps I did not have the strength to doubt him.

I thought of the vault. Centuries of Capulet bones lay there. Tybalt's body was there too, festering in his shroud. Did the spirits of the dead haunt their tombs at night? Would I wake to hear them screaming?

Nurse said the shrieks of the dead sent people mad. Would I go mad? Would I dance with Tybalt's body, as we had danced when I was small? Or take some kinsman's bone to be a weapon as I saw Tybalt's ghost seek out my Romeo? 'Stay, Tybalt!' I would cry. 'Romeo is mine. I will not let you hurt him!'

The thought of Romeo steadied me.

'Romeo, I come,' I whispered. 'This do I drink to thee.'

The poison tasted of swamps. Once again I felt strange: as if I saw myself in endless mirrors; as though I had done this a thousand times, a million.

I threw myself back upon the bed. Nurse would straighten any creases when they came to lay me out. I tried to think of Romeo, galloping on his horse from Mantua. I tried to imagine his strong arms about me, his warmth. When I woke, I would not be alone, but with my love.

But all I felt was darkness, and the cold, seeping through my blood.

# Chapter 22

I knew I was not dead because I dreamed. I dreamed of Romeo, galloping from Mantua, his horse all flecked with foam. There were tears upon his cheeks. Why was he weeping? We would be together now. He should be riding here with joy.

Noises, half-heard, and yet my body could not move. Even my eyelids were made of lead. My body, lying on something hard. Cold air, the smell of death.

I longed for dreams, but now I was not asleep, nor alive, nor dead. There were no dreams, no sound, no sight; nothing but the scent of flowers, meat and bone.

And then a voice. Romeo's voice, at last!

I had to move to meet it. I had to speak. But I could neither speak nor move.

'Oh, my love, my wife,' he whispered. 'Death, that hath sucked the honey of thy breath, hath had no power yet upon thy beauty ...'

Why did Romeo talk of death? Was he talking to Tybalt's corpse? I had to wake! I had to speak to him, to touch him! I could not.

'Here's to my love!' he whispered. 'Oh true apothecary! Thy drugs are quick. Thus with a kiss I die.'

I heard his words, half-dreaming. I felt his lips, so warm on mine. I tried to meet them, to lift my hand to his. I felt Romeo's body, beside me once again, his dear body, so near and so familiar. But my body would not move, not even for my love. The blackness held me, and the stench of bones.

And then, at last, I dreamed. I dreamed of a girl in love, standing on a balcony. I dreamed of the moon smiling on the rose garden. It was a good dream. I did not want to leave it. I would keep it to me, dream it as many times as the sky has stars. That girl's love would come to her. They would have two nights of love, one of whispered words and one of passion.

Slowly the dream faded, bringing back the darkness and the smell of bone.

I knew before I woke.

'Where is my Romeo?' My voice was a shadow's whisper, not my own.

And there he was. His face lay next to mine, just as I had dreamed it. I touched his lips with mine. They were warm. I stroked his face. His still face. I whispered, 'I am here. I am alive, my love.'

But Romeo was dead. I knew it before the friar told me so.

Friar Laurence stood next to me in the dark crypt, his face pale in the light of a single candle, his hands trembling, his mouth moving. He spoke as I lay there on the bier, hoping my body's warmth might seep into the cooling flesh of my husband. Gone, I thought. His light, his warmth. Our life together. Dead. Vaguely I heard the friar's words. Romeo had never got the message. He had galloped here, thinking I had died.

I thought: I should be screaming anguish. Should be tearing at my hair, my clothes. My wedding gown, dressed for Paris, worn in the tomb for my true husband. Romeo, my love.

The friar's voice was high and scared. 'He must have drunk poison. He must have stabbed the Earl to death too.'

So the friar had come to sit with me in case I woke in darkness. Instead of just a sleeping girl he found my dead husband, and the Earl of Paris, dead as well.

Words, words. So many words, filling the stinking tomb. Vaguely I was aware of bodies, bones, skulls and moss, the gabbling of the frightened friar. What did they matter? All my world was Romeo now. I sat up, then wished I hadn't. My body no longer felt my husband's next to mine. It felt wrong, to be even so little apart now. I pushed back my hair, trembling.

'Come.' The friar tugged at my hand. 'I'll dispose of thee among a sisterhood of holy nuns.'

I had an instant's image of myself in old age, kneeling among other nuns. My prayers would be worth nothing. Even then, in fifty years, a hundred, my thoughts would be of Romeo. There was no place for me in any convent.

I turned and took my loved one's hand. Already it was cool.

There was a noise outside. Men's voices. The guards must have seen the tomb unlocked, or someone had told them of a noise inside.

'The watch is coming!' the friar whispered. 'I dare no longer stay!'

Poor frightened friar. He had married us, plotted with us. Perhaps he would be banished, if his part in this was discovered.

My hope of ending the war between our houses had vanished with my Romeo. But the friar still had a life to live, out in the world. There was none for me. I could never inhabit the shell of the obedient daughter now.

'Then go,' I told him. 'Get thee hence, for I will not away!'

I heard the friar's footsteps running in the dark. Heard the scuttle of a rat. Once I would have screamed at that.

No use for plots now. There was nothing I could do or say to change this moment. My future, gone. The nights, warm with lovers' whispers, lost; the days, with laughter from our children, gone. I had lost not only the man I had wed but the man he would grow to be; my Romeo with a grey beard, and I with silver in my hair, wandering together down life's hill as we had climbed it together. Two great houses united because two lovers once their troth had plighted.

But my Romeo was dead. Our love was always of the night, with only the moon to give it life. And so love ended here, in the darkness of the tomb.

No. Love must not end! Nor could I bear to be taken from this tomb, away from Romeo. There was still one way we could be together ... in death. Our families would be married in their grief.

It was I who had challenged Romeo to marry me. Now I must have the courage to join him here forever.

I opened my love's fingers, took the poisoned cup from his grasp. I lifted it to drink. It was dry; no friendly drop left so I could die after he had drunk his fill.

I kissed his lips again. Cold lips. Sweet lips. No poison for me there.

Another noise outside. A man. Two men.

I lifted up Romeo's dagger. It was warm from his body, the only warmth left of him for me to know. I pressed it to my heart. Romeo, my love, I am the sheath for your dagger now.

The tip pierced the cloth of gold, then stopped. I pushed harder. The metal met flesh, then bone, and stopped. I felt a trickle of blood, cold as the tomb's air. How could it be so hard to kill a girl? Men killed other men each day. If they could do it, so could I.

I leaned down, till the dagger was between my heart and knees, then pushed down further. I felt the dagger resist, then slide.

The pain was ... pain. I had expected pain. I did not expect the cold. My toes, my face, my heart, were torn with ice; each breath as though a bullock weighed it down. The golden dress was wet with blood.

I took another breath, but could not find it. Shadows gathered at my eyes. I lay back upon the bier. I felt again the body of my husband. 'Romeo,' I whispered. 'I am here.' My fingers found his hand. Cold skin against cold skin. I shut my eyes, and felt him smile at me.

We seemed to fly, though still in darkness. Words drifted around us, from faces not yet here. My father, crying; Romeo's father, dressed in tears as well; his mother, dead of heartbreak; my mother, sobbing as her heart broke. Too late, I thought vaguely, they have learned they loved us. Too late they've learned in grief what they should have learned from love.

Enmity can vanish like the darkness once you look at what you share.

I knew it all, and yet knew nothing as my flesh grew cold like his.

Weep for us, my spirit cried, for never was there a story of more woe, than this of Juliet, dying with her Romeo.

# Chapter 23

## ROB

Jam lay in bloody puddles on the stage. Rob stood behind the curtain, waiting to go on. He would have to scrub the floor after the performance, as well as wash the jam and wine splodges from the costumes before he went to bed tonight.

His hand trembled on the curtain. Only a master actor could play this part. He was just a boy.

He could hear the audience muttering, the yell of an orange seller, the cracking of walnuts, the cries as friends greeted each other from the balconies. Nicholas strode across the stage as Romeo, plotting with Simon as Benvolio to sneak into the Capulets' ball.

The actors exited past him, into the wings. Simon patted Rob's cheek briefly as he passed. 'It's going well, lad. They liked the sword fight. You'll be right.'

Rob tried to nod. His cheeks felt hot under the white lead paint. Only the beetroot gave his lips and cheeks colour. His wig itched. His thick velvet dress was heavy, the whalebone so stiff he hoped he wouldn't trip. It stank too. A rat had made a nest in one of the costume trunks, and died when it was shut up.

His heart beat louder than a drum.

*Lady Capulet: Nurse, where's my daughter? Call her forth to me?*

*Nurse: Now, by my maidenhead — at twelve year old — I bade her come.*

He couldn't do it. They'd throw walnut shells at him. The play would close. The players would tramp the roads, like pedlars.

*Nurse: Where's this girl? What, Juliet?*

Terror bit him, gluing his silk slippers to the floor.

And suddenly she was there, or she was him, or he was her. It didn't matter. Somehow his feet became her feet. She glided onto the stage, her face downcast, her eyes glancing obediently at her mother.

'How now! Who calls?' His voice. Her voice.

The audience were silent, their nutcrackers and oyster knives forgotten on their laps.

And all at once he understood what Simon had told him during his first week with the company: 'Words are all very well, boy. But a true actor can bring the crowd to tears without a word. That is our mystery, lad. The playwright puts down the words. But the audience that watches — they're ours.'

You're mine, Rob thought. For these few moments, every lady, gentleman, servant or apprentice here belongs to me. And to her as well.

For Juliet was with him.

Somewhere, sometime, there had been a girl. Perhaps her name was even Juliet. It was her strength that drew in those gazes. And she was here today, in the words that he would say, in his every gesture, and in their minds, pleading for love to triumph over enmity.

He stood there, silent in the heavy dress, as Nurse and Lady Capulet went on and on and on, word after word. But no one muttered that the speeches were too long. No one even cracked a walnut. It was as though the audience already knew the end, the fate of this slight girl who stood with eyes downcast.

And you will weep for me, Rob thought. Each one of you. Even you men, sitting straight as broomsticks so your neighbours don't see your tears. Every day till you are dust, you will remember how you watched a young girl die in front of you, for love. There will be no actor in your memory, no theatre and no stage. Just the girl, the aching of her tears, the tears you shed for her, and for me.

She did not die. Cannot die, as long as actors tread the stage. Tomorrow and tomorrow and tomorrow, she soars above your webs of hate. Today, and in your memory forevermore.

I am Juliet.

# Author's Notes

Once there was a girl called Juliet.

Or was there? She probably existed. Shakespeare's play was based on other plays, which may also have been based on earlier works, and finally, perhaps, on a tale of what did happen to two young lovers, one called Juliet.

But even if every play was fiction, Juliet still lived. The story of a girl and boy in love despite their families' enmity is a story as old as humankind. It will happen time and time again as long as we humans feel love and hatred.

That is why the play still speaks to us. Wherever there is hatred, irrational and irreconcilable, there will be lovers desperate to hold hands across the chasm created by their families or their cultures, Romeos and Juliets.

Perhaps, one day, there will be a time when hatred withers and only love is left.

Three years ago, I spoke to a group of teenagers who were studying *Romeo and Juliet* at school. They hated it. 'All those words,' one of them said. Then they saw a movie version. They cried. They loved it.

Shakespeare's plays were written to be performed, with interludes of fighting, dancing, singing and performing bears. His plays are filled with jokes and puns we no longer understand. They weren't written to be read, with no action to leaven the long speeches.

Nor were they written in stone. Each time the play was performed — the company put on a different play each day — bits were changed, by the owner, the manager or by the actors, as I have made small changes for this book, changing some of the 'thee' and 'thou' to 'you' and 'your' as Shakespeare would do if he were putting on the play today. The text of *Romeo and Juliet* only became 'accepted' when Shakespeare's friends had his plays published after his death, in case they were forgotten.

The role of Juliet can be played in many ways. Mostly she is played as an innocent who has bad things happen to her. For most of the more than four hundred years since the play was written, women, and girls, have had little power over their own lives, or the world of men (women in Shakespeare's time belonged to men — a husband could even legally sell his wife at the market, though it seems to have been done rarely). But you can read her role differently. Juliet does the unthinkable for the time: she asks Romeo to marry her. She plots, she schemes; she has the courage to face almost death and a dark crypt, then real death, killing herself with a dagger.

*Romeo and Juliet* is one of Shakespeare's early plays, written when Queen Elizabeth I was alive. Did he create a strong heroine to please the Queen, just as he would create the evil Lady Macbeth and witches to delight her successor, King James I, who disliked powerful women? Or did Shakespeare himself dream of a girl with strength and love enough to end a feud, a girl like Juliet?


## ALL THOSE WORDS

Why did Shakespeare muck up a good story with so many words?

An easy answer is that the words are beautiful. But for modern readers, many of them are just ... well, too many. Why?

Shakespeare wrote what his audience would enjoy. So why didn't he make his plays the equivalent of a modern movie — few words and lots of action? Well, partly he did. His plays were written to be acted. The directions 'Fight' or 'Exit, pursued by a bear' don't look like much on the page. But a lot of the play's stage time was taken up with dances, fights and lovemaking.

There is one other aspect that is strange to modern readers and theatre-goers: well-educated people in Shakespeare's time were expected to speak wittily and poetically. Characters like the nurse or the servants could speak plainly, but not well-born girls like Juliet, or noble young men like Romeo. They were trained from an early age to speak 'lots of words', and very well indeed. Shakespeare's main characters are well-born men and women, girls and boys. To be realistic, they had to use 'all those words'.

This book cuts down those words, leaving only those spoken by Juliet or in Juliet's presence, as the story is told from her point of view. Even those words have been cut back a little in places, or clarified — for example, speaking of a rope ladder rather than a 'cord'. I don't think Shakespeare would have minded these changes. He might even have muttered something about cutting the cloth to suit the man. Shakespeare did his best to bring in the punters. I suspect he was content for anyone to add anything to his plays, or subtract it, as long as it brought more pennies slipping into the money box at the front door.

I also suspect he would have been horrified to see his plays made compulsory reading for teenagers in the classroom, without speech and colour and movement, or lighting and props. He wrote short sonnets to be read. A play was a performance piece.

Much of the dialogue in this book comes from the play. But Juliet lived in Shakespeare's imagination, and his mind would have been full of images long before he put her story down on paper. For that reason, I have sometimes given Juliet lines from other works by Shakespeare. I also based Paris's song to Juliet at the banquet on one of Shakespeare's sonnets; but where Shakespeare says his mistress is 'nothing like' a range of clichés, I have Paris declaring that Juliet is, turning a poem of wit and beauty into the trite verse Shakespeare was parodying.

## WHO WAS THE PLAY WRITTEN FOR?

Much has been written about how Shakespeare's plays were performed 'for the common man'. This isn't quite true. For the cost of a penny, anyone could stand in the 'pit' in front of the stage. These 'groundlings' in the cheap seats might throw rotten apples, or worse, oyster shells, if they didn't like the play. They had reason to complain. A penny back then — or two pennies, tuppence, if you wanted a seat; and possibly more for the higher boxes — was the equivalent of at least a hundred dollars or more now. Many could afford it, but they still wanted value for money: the latest fighting techniques from Italy with sword and dagger; the latest dances in the banquet scenes; and, if possible, a dancing bear or other spectacles.

*Romeo and Juliet* was never the equivalent of modern pop culture, appealing to people who didn't love words. You could pay a farthing, or even a 'mite' (four farthings, or eight mites, to a penny), to see street mummery, or the dancing bear by itself; or pay nothing at all to see a cock fight, bear-baiting, dog fights, freak shows and other entertainment — even a hanging. 'All those words' were never meant to be easy for everyone to understand. They were meant to be measured, clever and beautiful. Most of all they were meant to be listened to, not read. A good actor gives the words balance and meaning. The actions on stage break up the long speeches.

## TIME AND PLACE

*Romeo and Juliet* takes place in Verona, Italy, in the 1300s — but it also took place in London of the 1590s, as well as in Shakespeare's imagination and the imaginations of the actors who performed it, and they were very firmly located in Elizabethan England. This is where *I am Juliet* is set too.

*Romeo and Juliet* represents English values of the time, even if there are a few foreign flourishes, like the names 'Romeo' and 'Capulet'. Shakespeare knew little about Verona. I too know very little about Verona in the 1300s, or in these days either, but from the age of about ten I spent a large part of my imaginary life in Elizabethan England, and as an adult spent part of my professional life researching it.

*Romeo and Juliet* was probably written somewhere around 1591 to 1595, when Queen Elizabeth I was on the throne. By then, she was old for the times, and there was great uncertainty about who would reign after her, as she had never married and had no children. Nor had she named an heir.

Shakespeare's world was a dark and dangerous one. Before Elizabeth I's reign, England had been ripped apart by religious hatred. Elizabeth's father, Henry VIII, had declared England to be a Protestant country. On Henry's death, his son, Edward VI, kept the Church of England as the official religion, with the King as head of the Church. When King Edward died young, his sister Mary I declared that England was again Roman Catholic. Holding to your religion could cost you your life, because you were guilty of treason if you did not keep to the faith declared by your King or Queen.

The country was torn by political and religious warfare and hatred, as well as by feuds that may have begun with an insult, now long forgotten. In a time when men carried swords, rapiers, or at least a knife, even a small quarrel was often a deadly one.

This was also a land scarred by the bubonic plague, or Black Death, with one in three or four people dying in any outbreak. The theatres were shut during major outbreaks, and stayed shut for months or even years. Famines occurred as farm workers died, or merchants no longer brought goods to cities during bad plague years. In 1592, about the time *Romeo and Juliet* was written, perhaps ten per cent of the English population died of the plague in that single year.

Shakespeare's England, and especially London, was a place of civil strife, with large numbers of unemployed, and bad harvests leading to starvation. There was no police force, so young men fought openly in the streets with swords, knives and rapiers. The most popular entertainment was bear-baiting — a dog pitted against a bear; or dog fights, where dogs ripped each other to death. Great crowds gathered to enjoy public hangings or floggings, or to throw muck at figures in the stocks. London was a town of inns and taverns; of drunken brawls; of a river that stank and narrow streets where chamber-pots were emptied.

It was a time of fear, uncertainty and horror. It was also a time of love and beauty, courage and duty, of great hope and pride and laughter. No time is simple, nor any culture, and nor was Shakespeare's. But it helps you understand the play if you know a little of the way he, and the audience he wrote for, lived.

It was also a time when a woman had no power. A girl or woman was, quite literally, owned by her father or her husband. But it was also a time ruled over by a woman, and Elizabeth I was loved possibly more than any other English monarch before and since. In 1588, a few years before *Romeo and Juliet* was written, Elizabeth was credited with saving England from the Spanish Armada.

Shakespeare's theatre company regularly performed for the Queen. Possibly, she appreciated a play where a young girl — a virgin, like herself — took her destiny into her own hands: proposing marriage to Romeo, arranging the marriage, and refusing the plans of the male rulers, her father, her destined fiancé Paris and the Prince. *Romeo and Juliet* ends with Juliet — a young girl, and supposed to be powerless in Elizabethan times — triumphant, for she has kept the love she chose, even if it took her death to do it. The last words of the play are not 'Romeo, and his Juliet' but 'Juliet, and her Romeo'.

## THE HISTORY OF THE PLAY

Once, perhaps, there really were 'two households, both alike in dignity' with 'ancient grudge' breaking 'to new mutiny'. Shakespeare based his play on two earlier works: Arthur Brooke's 1562 poem *The Tragicall History of Romeus and Juliet*, which was in turn based on a French adaptation, by Pierre Boaistuau, of an Italian poem by Matteo Bandello; and a prose version, *Romeo and Juliet: the goodly Hystory of the true and constant Love between Rhomeo and Julietta*, that appeared in William Painter's 1567 collection of stories, *The Palace of Pleasure*. Shakespeare's *Romeo and Juliet* closely follows Brooke's poem, but he added a lot of extra drama and more and richer characters — and, of course, those words that actor Rob Goughe in this book complains about, and students complain about when they have to study them.

The story itself is much older. Masuccio Salernitano wrote a story called *Mariotto and Ganozza* in 1476, which has a similar plot — the warring families, the young lovers, the secret marriage — although he ends with the hero being beheaded for murder and the heroine dying of grief. Luigi da Porto adapted this story in *Giulietta e Romeo*, published in 1530. Both authors claimed the story was true.

Shakespeare's *Romeo and Juliet* was probably written sometime between 1591 and 1595. He may even have written several versions of it — quite likely if the initial performance was successful but he thought he could make it better still. As Shakespeare had his own theatre company, he had a large degree of freedom in what he chose to have performed, and probably also used the opportunity to improve his plays.

The versions of his plays that we know today were only published after his death, paid for by his friends. Unless an earlier manuscript turns up — possible, but unlikely — we have no way of knowing how much he rewrote his plays each time they were revived and performed again. We do know that he wrote quickly and easily — the foreword to the collection of plays published after his death says that Shakespeare wrote so fast he never stopped to blot the page — but did he ever rewrite his first drafts?

It would be a rare writer who didn't want to tinker with his work if he had the chance, and Shakespeare certainly had many chances to do so, especially when the London theatres were closed for so long during a severe outbreak of the plague. Although his theatre company may have performed out of London at that time, it's also likely that Shakespeare went back to Stratford-upon-Avon, where his wife and two daughters lived, and his son Hamnet who died in 1596, and where Shakespeare eventually retired, and possibly reworked his plays. But that is supposition. We know very little about Shakespeare's life, or about the way he worked, except for that line written by his friends.

*Romeo and Juliet* was published in 1597, edited by John Danter. Another version was printed in 1599 by

Thomas Creede: this one was about eight hundred lines longer and far better, but it lacked many of the stage directions that appeared in the first text. It's possible that the first edition was based on a copy of the play stolen by an actor, or even by Danter himself, taking notes as a member of the audience. But it's also possible, even probable, that the first printed version was what had first been performed, and that Shakespeare kept revising the work. Later editions would therefore have been Shakespeare's later drafts of the play.

## THE THEATRE AND ITS PLAYERS (ACTORS)

Theatres weren't allowed in the actual city of London because they encouraged people to gather and might spread the plague. The theatres and taverns where Shakespeare worked were all south of the river, in a rough area where other activities not allowed in the city also took place. We don't know when *Romeo and Juliet* was first performed, but it wouldn't have been at the famous Globe Theatre, because it wasn't built until 1599.

The Globe was built specifically to put on plays, instead of the actors having to use a pub's forecourt for a stage and audience area. The Globe's earliest stage was open to the sky; if it rained, there was no performance.

Women were not permitted to be actors. Until *Romeo and Juliet*, most women's parts were small, with older, experienced actors taking the main (male) roles. The first Juliet may have been played by John Heminges, an apprentice actor of about thirteen years old, his voice not yet broken. Another suggestion is the actor Robert Goffe (little else is known of him), who might or might not be the actor Robert Goughe, who died in 1624 and began his career as a boy player in about 1585, when the company was known as the Admiral's Men. Shakespeare was an actor as well as a theatre manager and playwright. He must have admired the ability of whoever was the first young actor to play Juliet to write him such a crucial part.

The leading players trained apprentices, but very little else is known about how acting was taught, or what sort of acting styles were in fashion. We do know that some actors specialised in tragic roles, and others were well known as fools or clowns. The leading players shared both the profits and costs of the company, but the minor players were paid a fee for each performance. If rain, or plague, meant no performance, no one made any money.

*Romeo and Juliet* was written when Shakespeare's company was known as Lord Hunsdon's Men. An actor in those days needed to be taken on as part of a lord's household, or he could be arrested as a vagrant.

This didn't mean the actors worked for Lord Hunsdon, just that they had been offered his protection and owed allegiance to his house.

## GROUNDLINGS

The 'groundlings' were people who bought the cheap tickets to the theatre and stood on the ground in front of the stage where there were no seats, though some patrons may have brought their own stools to sit on. A more expensive ticket gave you a seat in the covered areas, sheltered from wind and rain. When new theatres provided a covered stage, the groundlings — and the actors — could stay dry. The roof also allowed the players to use harnesses for tricks, like making the sprite Ariel in *The Tempest* fly.

## JULIET'S AGE

When the play opens, Juliet is two weeks from her fourteenth birthday. Despite Lady Capulet saying that girls Juliet's age were commonly married, this wasn't the case. Shakespeare's original audience would have known that thirteen was a very young age indeed to be married, or to have to make choices about marriage. Like us, they would have been shocked — but only slightly, as marriage at twelve was legal. But it was still unusual.

Although those of high rank, like royalty, or those who would inherit large fortunes, were married, or at least betrothed, when they were very young to cement alliances between families and countries, an eighteen-year-old woman was still considered young to be married. The best age for a woman to be wed was considered to be in her early twenties. Commoners married at an average age of twenty-two; noblewomen at an average age of about sixteen.

This was because most men weren't financially in a position to marry till they'd finished their apprenticeship and journeyman years and become a master of their trade, or had inherited family land to support a family — so were usually in their mid-twenties and often older. Women had to be old enough and experienced enough to manage a household.

So why did Shakespeare make his heroine so young? Juliet's youth meant she had less experience of the world outside her home than an older girl would have had. In Juliet's day, upper-class girls were kept within the seclusion of their family's home and under constant supervision until they were old enough to take part in formal social occasions. An older Juliet would have been less impulsive and better able to see other choices she might make, like life after Romeo's death.

Juliet was an heiress. Her marriage to Paris would have been a strategic alliance, between an aristocratic family (Paris is the Prince's cousin) and a wealthy house like the Capulets, who presumably were merchants as that was the main source of great wealth at the time. Other wealth came from the land: the nobility owned massive estates, which were worked by tenant farmers who paid rent and a share of the crops they grew to their lord.

In the play, Juliet's mother asks her merely to consider the marriage to Paris; and her father initially objects because she's so young. It's only Juliet's extreme grief after Tybalt's death that makes them think she would be happier married. Paris is repeatedly referred to as 'the young Paris' so he too would have been younger than most men were at the time of marriage. His genuine grief at Juliet's death shows he had truly fallen in love with her, or at least with what she looked like, or the wife he imagined she would be.

We're not told how old Romeo is. At the beginning of the play he declares his love for Rosaline, then changes to Juliet; and his family evidently hadn't yet made any marriage plans for him. He's probably not much older than Juliet.

Romeo and Juliet's tragedy wasn't just that they were lovers from warring families, but that such a young girl and boy were forced to make desperate decisions for themselves in order to escape a future being decided for them by others.

## ELIZABETHAN WEDDINGS

What we consider the traditional form of marriage — the bride in white, the vows at the altar — are relatively recent traditions. In Elizabethan times, a marriage could be far more informal: an agreement between two people, attested to by witnesses, with a separate sanctification by the church. While normally notice had to be given — a 'crying the banns' on three consecutive Sundays or 'holy days' in the parish church before the wedding on a Sunday, in case of objections — by Shakespeare's time a 'special licence' could be bought that would allow a couple to be married at once, if they also signed and paid for a marriage bond that asserted the marriage was lawful and neither party was married or betrothed to anyone else.

Presumably Romeo paid for a 'marriage bond' to marry Juliet. I haven't included it in the story, as Juliet wouldn't have known about it. Friar Laurence, however, would have pointed out the need to Romeo and even possibly arranged it.

Shakespeare would have known exactly how quickly — and quietly — a marriage could be arranged. He was married quickly, by marriage bond, to the pregnant and much older Anne Hathaway.

If Juliet had been formally betrothed to Paris, the marriage to Romeo may not have been legal. If the marriage to Romeo hadn't been consummated, it could have been quickly annulled. Only Friar Laurence could testify that the marriage had taken place. And only Juliet's nurse could testify that the marriage had been consummated. If Friar Laurence had torn up the marriage papers, there'd have been no proof that Romeo and Juliet were married. If the nurse had lied about the marriage being consummated, then Juliet's father could have applied for an annulment of her marriage to Romeo and married her to Paris instead. Juliet would have been powerless.

What would have happened then? Paris might not have wanted a bride who'd possibly been 'deflowered'. But the play makes the point repeatedly that Paris is young and loves Juliet, loves her so much he wants to be in her tomb. I suspect he would still have married her, hoping — expecting — that love would come with marriage and the position she would have enjoyed as his wife.

At some stage, Romeo would have been allowed to return to the city to take up his inheritance. Perhaps the enmity between the Montagues and Capulets would have got worse if Romeo saw his bride married to another. Or perhaps his love for Juliet would have been great enough to heal the rift, even if they were unable to marry each other again.

Perhaps each of them might even have been happy with their different wife or husband and their own children. They might have kept the memory of their teenage love to gaze at in private, and then put away and continue with their fulfilled lives. Happily ever after can happen, even after tragedy, although it didn't for Juliet and Romeo.

### WHAT MIGHT HAVE BEEN …

Would Romeo and Juliet have been happy together if they'd lived?

Probably. Even if they'd lived in exile for a short while, both families would have eventually forgiven them. Each family had only the one child.

The Prince, as the Juliet in this book realises, would have rejoiced that the two families were joined and the brawling and warfare had stopped. His city would have become even more prosperous with the alignment of the Capulets and the Montagues.

Romeo would have been an excellent heir for the House of Capulet; in the play, even Lord Capulet states to Tybalt that Romeo was known as a sober, industrious and good lad. The combined Montague/Capulet clan would have become even more wealthy and powerful.

Romeo and Juliet had similar backgrounds, wanted similar lives, and would continue to do so.

And they loved each other. Love at first sight exists. You can learn a lot from that first glance at someone: the subconscious recognises signals of a similar background, signs of laughter or kindness, and a hundred other signs that we may not be consciously aware of. We only know that we like, and love. I fell in love with my husband if not at first sight, then at the second, although it took a year before I cautiously accepted that this was, indeed, a love to base a lifetime on.

Love at first sight may not last. But a surprisingly large number of people do, in fact, fall in love pretty much at first sight, even if it is rash to rely on those feelings till you know more. Some people are very good at presenting a false face to the world, and you may mistake them for someone you should love. Others are good at pretending that the person in front of them is the person they *want* them to be, unable to see who is actually there.

Love can grow slowly, a deepening friendship. And love changes too. The love I felt for my husband a quarter of a century ago isn't the same as the richer love I feel for him now, though the memory of that first 'love with wings' is still part of it.

Romeo and Juliet's love would have changed, grown richer and more fulfilled, with children and a life together. And, yes, they would have been happy.

## WHO WAS FRIAR LAURENCE?

The decades before Shakespeare's birth had been tumultuous. King Henry VIII declared that England was no longer Roman Catholic and was now a Protestant nation. He closed down the monasteries and convents, and took their land and treasures for himself or those he favoured. His son Edward's brief reign had also favoured Protestants. Anyone who disagreed was guilty of treason, for the King was head of the Church as well as the country. Traitors were locked in the Tower of London or other prisons, tortured, hanged, beheaded and burned. Henry's daughter Mary I, whose reign followed Edward's, was staunchly Roman Catholic. Those who had become Protestant during the two previous reigns now became traitors, unless they changed their religion again. Once again the Mass was said in Latin. Those who disagreed with the return to Roman Catholicism were burned at the stake, earning the Queen the name 'Bloody Mary'.

Shakespeare grew up under the reign of Elizabeth I, who made England Protestant again. Those who remained Roman Catholic were regarded as potential traitors, and it was feared they might try to put the Catholic Mary Queen of Scots, Elizabeth's first cousin once removed, on the throne. Church services were changed to English again, not Latin. Shakespeare's father was at one time given the job of getting rid of all signs of what the English called 'Popery' in the Stratford church, including painting over the murals. But many older people, even if they were nominally members of the Church of England, would have felt comfortable with Roman Catholicism, the religion of their childhood.

England was still in transition from one form of Christianity to another, and I suspect this was the reason Shakespeare carefully didn't include a dramatisation of the wedding in *Romeo and Juliet*. His play is neither overtly Catholic nor Protestant. At the time it was being performed, Elizabeth I hadn't named her heir. While it was likely that King James of Scotland, a Protestant, would become King of England after Queen Elizabeth's death, Shakespeare would have known all too well that if the next monarch were a Roman Catholic, Protestant words on paper might be enough to have him convicted of treason and executed.

So there is no wedding service in the play, nor even a priest or a vicar. But we do have Friar Laurence. He may be there because the play is ostensibly set in Verona, which was Roman Catholic. But more likely he was one of the friars who took the oath of confirmation for the Church of England. As such, he'd have been allowed to perform weddings as well as keep his old title of 'friar'.

Juliet goes to confession, but a Protestant in the Elizabethan England of the 1590s would also have gone to confession. The difference between the Protestant and Roman Catholic practice of the time was that, for Protestants, confession was no longer a sacrament. In Shakespeare's time, the old customs and titles still mingled with the new. But Shakespeare was very careful not to be too specific about exactly which religion his characters followed.

## OBSCENITY

Modern audiences don't see *Romeo and Juliet* as erotica. The Elizabethan words are often explicitly sexual, but modern readers mostly don't realise what they refer to. They don't know how truly bawdy Mercutio's words are when he says, 'Now will he sit under a medlar tree, and wish his mistress were that kind of fruit as maids call medlars, when they laugh alone.' Most people probably don't know what a medlar is, or what the fruit looks like. And I'm not going to enlighten you. You'll have to find your own medlar tree, and sit under it when the fruit is ripe, and look up at the shape of it, then watch the fruit suddenly fall, to realise quite how rude Mercutio's speech is.

*Romeo and Juliet* is full of vulgar puns that modern audiences don't understand (Mercutio again: '... and quivering thigh, and the demesnes that there adjacent lie'), either because the meaning of the words has changed, or because we don't look for bawdiness in elaborate speech. Shakespeare didn't just talk about sex; he made it funny. His was a bawdy age, when sex was often joked about. Even Queen Elizabeth I, in her fifties, opened the front of her dress to below her waist before the Spanish ambassador, teasing him that she was 'hot'.

A sexual joke these days is referred to as a 'dirty joke'. In Elizabethan times, open discussion of sexual matters was acceptable. Although these days a woman can expose her knees without being thought a loose woman, and advertisers use sex to sell everything from soft drinks to tight jeans, talking about sex is far more taboo today than it was back then.

This book is far less erotic than the play. I wanted it to be about the girl, not sex. Sex has a habit of taking over both books and lives, as it did for Romeo and Juliet. If their passion for each other had been less urgent, they might have lived.

In the play *Romeo and Juliet*, a thirteen-year-old girl marries and has the physical relationship that comes with marriage. That too is a taboo in our culture. Shakespeare had far more freedom to write about his lovers than I do.

Marie de France was a real person, a writer or singer of tales, some that she may have learned, others that she may have made up or retold in her own words. She lived and sang, or told, her stories in about the twelfth century, but nothing else is known of her; not where she lived nor even her true name. 'France' back then may have meant she came from the Île de France, now part of Paris. Or Marie might not have been French at all, but was given that name because she told tales from Brittany and France. Marie was the most common of names back then, and might even have been an alias.

Her stories were often passionate, which made them different from the more common morality tales, in which the more abuse a woman accepted from her husband, the more virtuous she was. Marie's stories may have given women more interesting roles than did others of her time, but as in the tale of Guigemar, her heroines were still often nameless. As Marie herself still is.

## ELIZABETHAN POISONS AND REMEDIES

Do not try the poisons or remedies in this book. Even the rue in Juliet's poison 'remedy' is toxic. The lead-based cosmetics, or the eye drops that made Elizabethan women's eyes look larger and shine brightly, were often deadly; and the remedies for their poisons were usually based on superstition, not science. Most Elizabethans led short lives. Even their poisons were not reliable: the toxicity and other properties of plants vary according to where and how they were grown, and prepared and stored.

## ELIZABETHAN FOOD AND DRINK

For the poor, food was whatever they could scavenge: bread when they could afford it; cheese, if possible; sometimes butter or milk; salt cod or other dried fish; and meat as a luxury. The rural poor ate pottage, which was a thick soup made of grain or dried peas stewed with green vegetables or weeds like nettles.

Fruits and vegetables were only available when in season, and included apples, pears, quinces, medlars, parsnips, turnips, peas, broad beans, celery, skirret, sea kale, radishes, onions, wild garlic and cabbages; nuts like walnuts and chestnuts; and a range of salad greens and edible flowers. Wild foods, like blackberries, burdock, dandelions, bilberries, hazelnuts, sloes, nettles, saltwort, sorrel, edible seaweeds and shellfish, were gathered too. Potatoes, tomatoes, zucchini, broccoli, pumpkins, fat orange carrots and many other fruits and vegetables we now take for granted had not yet been brought to

England in Shakespeare's time. The end of winter and the beginning of spring was 'the hungry gap', when stored food had been used up and the early harvest hadn't yet begun. At this time, an onion might be a luxury. In wealthy households, gardeners 'forced' asparagus spears or young celery to grow fast in beds of hot manure.

To us today, 'food' can mean a wide range of dishes, but for an Elizabethan it meant bread and meat first, pease pudding, and fresh or dried fish. For snacks, they would eat raw nuts, or roasted chestnuts in autumn and winter; oysters, winkles, mussels; apples bought hot and baked from the apple seller; pickled crabapples; radishes by themselves or with butter; or a crust of bread dipped in ale.

Two cooked meals were eaten each day, if you could afford them. Servants and those who did heavy work ate bread, perhaps with butter or cheese or leftover cold meat, when they first woke up. They would also drink ale, which might be heated in winter and have bread sopped in it. Dinner was the main meal, eaten at noon, with a smaller supper at dusk. Nobles and the wealthy ate dinner earlier, at about 11 am (their leftovers would feed their servants), and had supper earlier too. A banquet might begin at midday or mid-afternoon and continue for many hours with various courses, with music or dancing in between some of the later courses until they turned into 'supper'.

'Courses' weren't a single main dish with vegetables or salad, as we're used to today. A course might involve many different roasts, sweet dishes, and pies garnished possibly with fruit or vegetables, all on the table at once. Each course offered a different choice — roast venison instead of roast lamb or mutton, for example, or roast pigeon instead of roast duck. The final course at a banquet would often be mostly sweet foods, especially those made by the ladies of the house out of vastly expensive sugar: preserved cherries, stewed quinces, medlar paste, tiny marzipan figures coloured with vegetable juices and decorated with gold leaf. But even this final course might have meat dishes too, sweet ones like chopped spiced chicken with sugar, or fish cooked with honey and apples. At more simple dinners, the last course might be cheese and stewed fruit or a fruit pie, or a dish made of grated cheese sweetened with sugar and spiced with herbs.

Meat, and lots of it, was a sign of both wealth and strength. White bread was a luxury, and came in many shapes and flavours. Pies were common, but only as containers for their filling (only the poor bothered to eat the tough pastry). A 'humble pie' was a pie made of 'humbles' or deer entrails, well spiced.

The Elizabethans drank an enormous amount of alcohol. Low-alcohol ale was preferred over water as it had the advantage of not giving you the runs or killing you. Much 'fresh' water from wells was polluted by sewage, as were rivers or streams. Wine was drunk in wealthy houses, even by children, usually with a lot of water added. In a life filled with pain and hardship, even if you were wealthy, drunkenness was prized.

When you look at many of the stupider events of the last five hundred years of history, it is useful to remember that many or most of the participants were probably drunk. Lord Capulet's rage when Juliet refuses to marry Paris is more explicable once you realise that during the night spent sitting with Tybalt's corpse (as duty required) he had probably refreshed himself regularly with brandy. By the time he spoke to his daughter he would have been exhausted and very drunk indeed. The audience would know this and expect it. That was their world.

## ELIZABETHAN TABLE MANNERS

A place setting at a formal meal would have a plate (not the trenchers of bread more common in earlier times), a spoon and probably a knife. Forks were a new fashion, arrived from Italy, but even the most fashionable people were only just beginning to learn to use them. Men carried knives as a matter of course, and might use them to cut their food as well as to dispatch an enemy. A knife sometimes had prongs or a prong on one end to help in picking up food from the common dish. But usually food arrived at the table already in pieces that could be eaten with the fingers or a spoon, or as great joints that were carved at the table.

In simple households, the male head of the house would carry out the carving. In wealthier homes, it might be done by a professional carver, who would also add sauces or seasoning to the pieces he had carved.

A spoon might be hand-carved wood, or silver, or an alloy of gold, depending on your status. A sucket spoon was a small spoon with a hollow handle used to eat moist sweet dishes, like stewed quinces.

Most Elizabethans used their fingers to pick up their food. Washing your hands before a meal, and wiping your fingers during it, was an important part of table etiquette. A host provided a basin and jugs of warm or scented water for their guests before they sat at the table. There would be bowls of scented water on the table to dip your fingers into during the meal, before drying them on the tablecloth or linen napkins.

The servants would serve wine or ale into the cups (wood, tin, pottery or expensive glass, or pewter, brass, silver or gold) at the sideboard, then serve each person individually; or the women of the household would serve the men. Food was put on the table for everyone to help themselves to. It wasn't good manners to reach across the table. You waited for your neighbour to ask if they could help you to a dish, or you asked for some of it, though the latter wasn't acceptable for a woman or a young person. Nor was it good manners to pick the most delicious bit for yourself, to wipe your face with your hand or sleeve, to dip your sleeve into the stewed apple or sauce, or brush it against the roast. If you didn't have the grace to make your long sleeves fall away from your wrists, it was best to discreetly pin them back before you helped yourself to food.

The wealthier you were, the more food you had in front of you. You weren't expected to eat it all, or even to taste each dish. In a household like the Capulets', the servants would eat the family's leftovers. In the royal household, royalty ate first, and it was an honour to eat the leftovers from the royal table.

## TRANSPORT

Few people had carriages at the time when *Romeo and Juliet* was first performed; nor were most of the narrow roads suitable for carriages to travel on. People rode horses, donkeys or mules; or were carried in chairs, or in litters where they lay on cushions.

## HAIRSTYLES

A young Elizabethan girl of good family wore her hair loose, perhaps with the hair next to her face plaited and drawn back, and decorated with flowers or jewels. A married woman swept her hair up into a bun or other style, and covered it with a veil, wimple, hairnet, hat or cap, depending on who she was and what she might be doing. A servant's hair might also be covered. A poorer woman might keep her hair covered much of the time to try to keep it lice-free.

## ELIZABETHAN COLOURS

The poor wore dull colours, and the rich wore bright ones. The richer you were, the brighter your clothes, unless you wore black for mourning. The dyes came from insects, lichens and plants, and were costly. Most dyes faded quickly.

Bright pink was a popular colour for men as well as women. Only royalty or those closely related to royalty, like Paris, were allowed to wear gold or silver, although the law was often disobeyed.

## THE BANQUET SONG

This is taken from Thomas Morley's *First Book of Ballets* (1595). The song in *I am Juliet* has been changed slightly to fit the scene. This is the original:

*Now is the month of maying,*
*When merry lads are playing, fa la,*
*Each with his bonny lass*
*Upon the greeny grass.*
*Fa la la! Fa la lala, la la.*

*The Spring, clad all in gladness,*
*Doth laugh at Winter's sadness, fa la,*
*And to the bagpipe's sound*
*The nymphs tread out their ground.*
*Fa la la! Fa la lala, la la.*

## SHAKESPEARE'S SONNET 130

Paris's song in the banquet scene of *I am Juliet* is meant to be the kind of song Shakespeare lampooned in this poem. Well-born men composed poetry, songs and music, and would perform in company, partly as entertainment, and sometimes, probably, to show off their wit and cleverness. The explicitness of Paris's song — and his making such an open claim on Juliet in public — would be insulting today, but expected in the 1590s.

*My mistress' eyes are nothing like the sun;*
*Coral is far more red than her lips' red;*
*If snow be white, why then her breasts are dun;*

*If hairs be wires, black wires grow on her head.*
*I have seen roses damasked, red and white,*
*But no such roses see I in her cheeks;*
*And in some perfumes is there more delight*
*Than in the breath that from my mistress reeks.*
*I love to hear her speak, yet well I know*
*That music hath a far more pleasing sound;*
*I grant I never saw a goddess go;*
*My mistress, when she walks, treads on the ground:*
*And yet, by heaven, I think my love as rare*
*As any she belied with false compare.*

# Acknowledgements

A manuscript is sometimes like an almost made cake, with still a bit of mixing, as well as baking and icing to be done.

*I am Juliet* was remixed as well as spiced by the superb editing of Nicola O'Shea, who smoothed out the lumpy bits where the combination of Shakespearean and modern language didn't quite mesh, the whole guided and shaped by the wonderful Kate Burnitt of HarperCollins.

Lisa Berryman as always gave me the confidence to contemplate a marriage of my words and Shakespeare's (I didn't realise until I was well into it how ambitious a task it would be). Lisa calmly beheaded the book, removing the last unnecessary chapter. When I lack the courage or clarity to evaluate my work, Lisa is there. She shared the planning of the next two books in this series: *Ophelia, Queen of Denmark* (2015) and *Third Witch* (2016). As always, there are no words enough to thank her.

Enormous gratitude to Angela Marshall, for yet again taking a mess of badly spelled words and turning them into a readable manuscript, and in this case, sharing her knowledge and love of the play to help fit text with the book.

To the teenagers who first inspired this book, complaining about *Romeo and Juliet*'s unrealistically long speeches: I hope by now you have travelled far beyond the teacher who discouraged you from expressing what were well thought out and valid opinions, even if you hadn't been taught how to transfer them to a page. With luck you have discovered that most teachers are not like yours (I eavesdropped on your teacher's conversation in the staffroom, and was grateful yet again that I was blessed with superb teachers, not ones who muttered, 'I don't know why we turn up, really' — I'm not sure why they turned up either). I hope you have found teachers with enthusiasm, insight and compassion. But if you haven't, and if you did leave school, thinking there was no point staying any longer: you are not stupid, despite your teacher's claims. If you still need to know how to write an essay: just write it down, exactly as you told me. I hope you will seize the most wonderful of futures, and perhaps even look again at Shakespeare and find beauty in his words.

And — belatedly — to the Brisbane Arts Theatre of my youth, who gave a teenager the privilege of playing third witch in *Macbeth*. One of my most treasured teenage memories is of sitting on a pile of scenery, dressed in black robes, warts and hunchback, studying for the next day's economics exam while Banquo in red velvet breeches lectured me on Marxist economics (I just wanted to work out how to calculate GNP). Without the Arts Theatre, and the magic of feet upon the stage, I too might have thought that Shakespeare was just 'all those words'.

**Jackie French AM** is an award-winning writer, wombat negotiator, the Australian Children's Laureate for 2014–2015 and the 2015 Senior Australian of the Year. She is regarded as one of Australia's most popular children's authors and writes across all genres — from picture books, history, fantasy, ecology and sci-fi to her much loved historical fiction. 'Share a Story' is the primary philosophy behind Jackie's two-year term as Laureate.

jackiefrench.com.au
facebook.com/authorjackiefrench